"Do you think make a good husband?"

Con's question almost made Verna choke on her drink. "Oh, you'd make a terrific husband. What wife could object to a man who cooks, cleans and does laundry?"

His eyes narrowed speculatively. "I did ask seriously. But okay—how would *you* fancy me as a husband, Verna?"

She hid her feelings beautifully, she thought. "If I were looking for a husband, which I most emphatically am not, I'd put you at the top of the list. Seriously."

"And why aren't you looking for a husband?" he asked in concerned tones. "You're not getting any younger."

"I've got plenty of time," Verna replied. "And besides, I'm very happy with my career."

And besides, she thought, *if I can't marry you, no one else will ever do....*

WELCOME
TO THE WONDERFUL WORLD
OF *Harlequin Romances*

Interesting, informative and entertaining,
each Harlequin Romance portrays an appealing
and original love story. With a varied array
of settings, we may lure you on an African safari,
to a quaint Welsh village, or an exotic Riviera
location—anywhere and everywhere that adventurous
men and women fall in love.

As publishers of Harlequin Romances, we're
extremely proud of our books. Since 1949,
Harlequin Enterprises has built its publishing
reputation on the solid base of quality and
originality. Our stories are the most popular
paperback romances sold in North America; every
month, six new titles are released and sold at
nearly every book-selling store in Canada and the
United States.

A free catalogue listing all Harlequin Romances
can be yours by writing to the

HARLEQUIN READER SERVICE,
(In the U.S.) 1440 South Priest Drive, Tempe, AZ 85281
(In Canada) Stratford, Ontario, Canada N5A 6W2

We sincerely hope you enjoy reading
this Harlequin Romance.

Yours truly,

THE PUBLISHERS
Harlequin Romances

The Sugar Dragon

by

VICTORIA GORDON

Harlequin Books

TORONTO • LONDON • LOS ANGELES • AMSTERDAM
SYDNEY • HAMBURG • PARIS • STOCKHOLM • ATHENS • TOKYO

Original hardcover edition published in 1980
by Mills & Boon Limited

ISBN 0-373-02427-4

Harlequin edition published September 1981

CHAPTER ONE

THE sands of Kelly's Beach shimmered like salt in the dying light of a pale, falling moon, and the soft-breaking Queensland surf caressed Verna Grant's bare feet as it whisked and rolled to erase her slow-paced footsteps behind her. Ahead, a rollicking black shadow marked the progress of her dog Sheba, but Verna was far too deep in her own thoughts to keep track of the dog's joyous roaming.

It was four o'clock in the morning, just five hours before she'd be gearing up to start her first day as editor of the weekly *Bundaberg Drum*. Any sensible woman would be home sleeping, but that pleasure had eluded Verna already for most of the night and she was too keyed up to bother trying again. It was silly and she knew it; after nearly ten years as a working journalist she had nothing to fear about handling her first legitimate post as editor. In fact she was quite looking forward to the challenge ... and the hard work that would keep her from thinking too often of Stephen. No, she wouldn't think about Stephen, Verna told herself angrily. It would be stupid and self-destructive to waste her thoughts on the likes of him. A liar and a cheat —a *married* liar and cheat who'd come within a whisker of making her the biggest fool ever.

She should have paid more attention to Sheba from the start. The cross-bred black bitch had never liked Stephen, not even in the beginning, which in retrospect seemed a terribly important omen. And even though Verna knew it was ridiculous to expect human judgments from an eighteen-month-old dog, she made a silent vow to pay more attention to Sheba's reactions next time.

'If there ever is a next time,' she muttered to herself, shaking her long, reddish-blonde hair in rueful anger. Her self-esteem had taken an awful bruising, but she wouldn't be able to let it affect her professional esteem, and she knew it. And what's a little self-esteem? she thought. Everything else is intact, for whatever that's worth. And it must be worth something, if only in terms of sheer rarity; after all, twenty-eight-year-old virgins could hardly be considered a glut on the market.

Lost in her thoughts, she veered more deeply into the soothing waves, and it wasn't until the tangy salt water splashed across her knees that she shook herself out of her reverie, if only a bit. Looking down at the waves, her eyes traced along slender legs that she knew were shapely and attractive, and the body above them was equally so, as was the face that she couldn't personally see as beautiful, but could accept as intriguing to the majority of men.

Verna had good, regular features over a fine, classic bone structure that, like her grandmother's, would wear very well indeed. Her hair was a reddish-blonde, almost sorrel colour that would probably bleach out to honey tones in the strong Queensland sun. Her eyes were exceptionally large and vibrant in a mix of bluey-green that altered with her moods. Bedroom eyes, she'd been told, flashing their greenest when she was aroused. Stephen—damn, damn, damn his soul to hell, she thought—had loved them, vowing they'd be even greener when she finally ...

But here, now, on a dark and deserted beach in the quiet hour before dawn, Verna knew they'd be their bluest, which was just as well, thank you. She could leave any arousing until later, much later, if at all. The last thing she needed was another man in her life. She had a new and exciting job, far from Melbourne's four-seasons-a-day climate and Stephen; she had her tidy little beach house with its broad sunporch and high-fenced yard; she had her slightly ageing purple Mini S; and she had Sheba, who wouldn't think of betraying her.

Verna shook her head angrily, trying to ignore the single tear she could feel trickling down one cheek. Being a twenty-eight-year-old virgin wasn't all that bad after all, she thought. She had everything she really needed and no need to share it with any selfish, insensitive, chauvinistic brute of a man.

To hell with them all, she vowed silently. If I make it through to thirty I'll stay a virgin until I die, and they can bury me under a spinster's tombstone—Returned Unopened. For some reason the irreverence of that bit of masculine chauvinism struck Verna as hilariously funny, and her laughter tinkled through the silence of the deserted setting.

But it wasn't the echo of her laughter that floated back to her. It was a harsh, masculine voice shouting a stream of abuse. The least offensive part of it was '... bloody great mongrel black bastard!' and Verna looked up in surprise to see Sheba's inky shape streaking along the beach toward her. Sheba's shape, and yet different somehow ... and when the dog got close enough Verna could see why. Sheba was prancing with her head high in the air, her jaws clamped tightly on the waistband of a pair of trousers. Trousers? Indeed they were, and the sight provided an instant explanation for the shouting that grew louder as Verna chased forward after the dog.

'Sheba! You come here!' she shouted as the darting black shape made an abrupt turn and sped off ahead of her. 'Sheba! You come back here ... *now*!'

She might as well have talked to the wind. Sheba thought

it a marvellous game, and when Verna finally reached the
site of the pilferage, clearly marked by a towel and a pair of
sandals, Sheba was a discreet and totally safe distance
ahead of her.

The dog's tongue lolled over the waistband of the slacks,
and as Verna stepped toward her again she threw her great
head into the air and leaped away joyfully.

'Oh ... no!' Verna sighed aloud as she saw a wallet and
a handful of coins shower from the pockets of Sheba's prize.
'Come here, you bad dog! Come here right this minute or
I'll thrash you within an inch of your life!'

'And it'll be a damned short life if I have anything to do
with it,' said a harsh voice from the water. 'Now you might
just stop shouting at the stupid bloody dog and do something about getting my pants back, if you don't mind.' The
voice seemed quite disembodied, and Verna had to look
carefully to see the head it belonged to, suspended in the
waves like some wayward ball.

'Well, I'm doing the best I can,' she replied angrily. 'But
obviously I can't catch her, can I? So you'll just have to be
a little patient.'

'It'll be too late for patience if it gets too much lighter,'
said the voice, raising into outrage as the gambolling dog
plunged into the edge of the breakers with the pants legs
dragging along beside her.

'Well, why don't you come out and help me?' Verna
shouted, suddenly knowing the reason even as he began
to wade closer in a strange, ominous silence.

She couldn't see his face in the half-light, but the body
that reared up from the waves was exquisitely, intensely
male. And very nice, too, she thought idly.

Broad shoulders tapered down to a muscular, narrow
waist, and the moonlight rippled on muscles in huge, powerful arms as he moved through the water. She stood for an

instant, drinking in the sight, then suddenly cried, 'No! Stay there!' as she realised how nearly clear of the water he was.

'What's the matter ... are you shy?' he growled. But at least he stopped, even if it was only one pace short of decency. Verna stood her ground as the waters lapped against his hips, her attention totally removed from her playful dog as she admired the man's splendid body.

The two of them stared at each other for a moment that went on for ever, and Verna found herself wondering if he was wondering about her face just as she wondered about his. If they stayed much longer, she realised, the wondering would be gone with the ebbing moonlight as dawn lapped against the watery horizon. Then something brushed against her bare leg, but even as she lunged downward Sheba danced away with the soaking trousers still firm in her jaws and the man's muffled curse ringing across the water.

'I'd have had her if you hadn't shouted,' she said with unexpected calmness, ignoring the obscene reply. 'Why don't you just go for another swim or something; she'll come to me again in a minute.'

'I've had my swim,' he replied in an icy voice.

'Well, I suggest you have another one,' Verna replied. 'And please stop cursing; it isn't going to help anything.'

'... bloody mongrel,' he replied.

'She's not a mongrel. She's a pure-bred Boxador,' Verna retorted. 'And she's normally a very well-behaved dog, as well. I expect if you hadn't shouted at her she'd have already come back. She thinks we're playing with her.'

'I'll play with her all right—with a rifle in my hand,' he snarled. 'And what the hell's a Boxador?'

'Half Boxer and half Labrador,' Verna replied smugly. 'Pure-bred on both sides, you see?'

'Pure mongrel and she ought to be shot,' he snarled back at her. 'Look out now, she's coming close again!'

At the sound, Sheba turned and danced away, leaving Verna to snarl her own reply. 'See! If you'd just keep quiet I'd have her. Now please shut up, and I'll see about picking up your wallet and money before she decides to run off with them as well.'

'Yeah, well, see if you can leave me the personal papers in the wallet,' he sneered. 'You can have the money if you'll just catch your damned dog and get out of here.'

Verna caught her breath at the innuendo, but he continued before she could speak. 'Pity you didn't train her better; you could have been gone with the money before I even noticed you'd been here.'

'Hah! Got you, you little black devil!' Verna cried, lunging down to get a tenuous but sufficient grip on Sheba's chain-link collar. Hanging on tightly, she squatted down and hauled the panting dog round to face her. 'You're a naughty, naughty little dog,' she scolded, holding out a hand. 'Now give me those trousers. Come on, give!'

And like an honours graduate of obedience school, the chocolate-coloured muzzle opened to place the sodden mess in Verna's outstretched hand.

'That's a good girl,' she crooned, rising to her feet with the soaked trousers held at arm's length. And then, 'No! Oh, no, Sheba ... damn it!' she cried as the black shadow homed in on the towel and flashed off down the beach with it, headed for home and no games this time.

'That's a good girl,' came the muttered sarcasm from the dripping figure in the waves. 'Hell! As a dog trainer you make a bloody good plumber, lady. Why didn't you hang on to her while you had the chance?'

'Because I didn't think she'd ...'

'I doubt if you'd know how to think,' he interjected. 'Now

would you like to put down my trousers and get those lovely long legs chasing after that little black menace so that I can get out of here before the sun comes up?'

Verna didn't know why she did it, but instead of dropping the trousers she moved with exaggerated slowness to where his wallet lay half buried in the sand. 'I'd better get the money first,' she replied hotly. 'Although I suppose it'll hardly be worth the trouble; from the look of these pants you're not likely to be rich.' Certainly the soaked and well-worn jeans didn't look very impressive, but she got her reward from the gasp of anger that exploded from the shadowy figure in the water.

'Bloody hell!' he cried. 'Haven't you done enough already?'

'You're swearing again,' Verna replied calmly. 'And I've asked you once before to stop it. Don't you know it isn't polite to use language like that in front of a lady?'

'Lady ... hell! You're nothing but a common thief, the route you're going. I'll bet you *have* trained that bloody dog, after all.'

Verna dropped the trousers in a sodden heap at her feet and made a great pretence of opening the wallet and extracting the notes from it. In the dim light, she knew the man wouldn't ever be able to tell that she wasn't really taking anything. 'Humph, just as I thought,' she shouted at him. 'Almost a complete waste of time.'

'I don't usually need a lot on the beach at this time of the morning,' he sneered. 'Now are you going to get out of here, or are you waiting for me to go home and fetch you some more money?'

'What a splendid idea,' Verna cooed sarcastically, now quite enjoying her game. 'Shall I call Sheba back so you can dry yourself first, or will you just drip-dry?'

There are very few words a female journalist gets through

ten years without hearing, but the shadowy figure in the water managed three that were brand-new to Verna, along with several she'd heard and would rather not have again.

'Just be thankful I haven't any soap with me,' she snapped when he'd run down, 'or I'd make you wash out your mouth while you're there. It's not much wonder you're so poor, with a vocabulary like that!'

'All right, I'm sorry, I apologise,' he said in a subdued voice, but the waves carried the 'bitch' he muttered after it, and Verna laughed at him.

'Naughty, naughty,' she chuckled, and then looked pointedly at the now-distant horizon. 'My, it's going to be very light soon, isn't it? Maybe I'll just take these old rags off for Sheba to play with later.' She didn't take her eyes from him as she knelt to retrieve the trousers, and for a second she wished it was light enough to see his face. She had an impression of thick dark hair, but with the light behind him she couldn't make out his features at all.

The shadows might obscure his features, but they served only to enhance the play of muscles across his lean but broad-shouldered torso, and Verna allowed herself one final assessment before she abandoned the game. Her eyes strolled slowly across his shoulders, caressing the hard lines that narrowed to the trim waistline. She looked at the rippling muscles of his upper arms and then moved her gaze further down to where the shadows played along narrowed hips and massive thighs. Thighs? She went rigid with shock for a second as she suddenly realised what was happening; then her voice broke into a shrill shriek. 'You ... you stay in the water ... oh ... no!'

The trousers seemed to burn her fingers and she dropped them in a heap as she turned and fled down the beach, running swiftly in the packed sand at the water's edge. There was a drumming sound in her ears, but even as a clasp of iron closed on her shoulder, she realised that he couldn't possibly have stopped to pick up his trousers.

She closed her eyes tightly as she struggled vainly against a grip that seemed to go right to the bone, and she didn't even hear herself crying, 'I'm sorry ... I'm sorry. Please don't ...'

'Please don't what?' said a harsh voice in her ear. 'I know what I'd damned well like to do with you, about now!'

His fingers burned at her shoulders as he turned her to face him, and Verna squinched her eyes even tighter. 'Oh no, you couldn't,' she squeaked as he pulled her so close against him that she could feel the heat of his body through her thin T-shirt and faded, well-worn shorts. Then his knee was forcing its way between her thighs as he crushed his arms around her.

'And why couldn't I?' whispered a voice like ice in her ears, and Verna shivered in terror at the menace it contained.

'Because I'm a virgin,' she whimpered, flinching at the raucous laughter the confession evoked. It jarred in her ears, a curious mixture of anger and jeering maddening disbelief.

'A virgin ... hah!' the chill voice sneered. 'How old are you?'

'T-t-twenty-eight,' Verna gasped, hardly able to breathe in her terror.

For an instant the hands seemed to lessen their iron grip on her shoulders, but then they tightened again and Verna's fears erupted in a scream for the only safety she could think of. 'Sheba! Sheba! Oh ... please!'

Her voice ranged from the initial shrillness to a whimper as the laughter grew in her ears. Then he stopped laughing and she was astonished to hear the snuffling, panting sound of her dog as it brushed against her legs.

'Oh God,' she thought. 'What are you doing, you stupid dog?' And as if in answer, the voice grated in her ear with maddening confidence.

'She's licking my feet ... have a look,' he said, and Verna almost opened her eyes before she realised she was being baited by this enormous, naked stranger whose voice throbbed through her as fully as did the warmth of his body.

'A twenty-eight-year-old virgin, eh?' he whispered almost whimsically. But the sudden softness of his voice didn't extend to the iron bands that held her to him, squashing her breasts against his chest and her thighs against the rigid pillars of his legs. Quite illogically, Verna was also aware of Sheba's tail beating against her own bare legs, and she realised that the demented, traitorous dog was indeed being friendly to this hulking, threatening stranger.

Then that insidious voice was speaking again, whispering into her ear the delights he planned for her, and Verna began to struggle against him, opening her mouth to scream out her terror. But instead his own mouth descended to smother her cries, burning her lips in a kiss that was like nothing she'd ever experienced. Stephen had been experienced, but his kisses were mild as dish-soap compared to the searing torture that seemed to flow through her in a growing, shattering wave of passion and searching.

Her lips parted beneath the assault and as he ravaged her with his mouth, those massive arms clamped her so closely against him that she felt as if she would melt right into his body. She struggled, but to no avail, and finally all of her resistance poured away from her, as his kiss seemed somehow to change, to lose its harshness and replace it with a growing tenderness. She didn't realise her arms had wound themselves around his neck until she felt tendrils of his hair within her fingers, didn't realise the vulnerability of his own upright stance until she felt his knee flex between her thighs and knew she could fight back ... if she had to. Or if she wanted to, because she also knew somehow that he wasn't about to rape her, either, but she didn't know why she knew it.

His lips moved even more tenderly across her mouth, and without thinking, Verna opened her eyes. But all she could see was his hair, coffee-brown in the hazy but strengthening dawn, and then his lips moved to caress her ear and the point of her jawline.

'Are you really a virgin?' The whisper seemed to come from nowhere and yet surround her, and Verna couldn't voice a reply. She did manage to nod her head, however, and the voice seemed to understand. 'That's rare,' the voice sighed. 'Too rare for me. Close your eyes.'

She did, without thinking to argue even had she been able to speak.

Sheba's panting seemed incongruously loud in the sudden silence that followed, and Verna could feel her own heart as it tried to batter itself free of her body. The bands around her eased slightly, and she took a hiccuping, shaky breath that sent shivers through her entire body. And then the voice soothed into her ear again.

'If you've kept it this long, it must be very valuable to you,' came the words. 'Cherish it ... rare things ought to be cherished.'

There was a long silence, and then Verna felt his lips touch her forehead, so gentle, so lightly that she almost couldn't feel them at all, but only the branding they left.

'Keep your eyes closed,' he whispered. And then his arms freed her, leaving her to stand in shaken, trembling wonder as her ears rang to the caress of his voice and the thunder of his retreating footsteps. Two voices shouted in her head —one saying open your eyes and look and the other saying close your eyes. And when she finally did look, he was only a shadow shape, far down the beach, and even that was blurred by the tears she couldn't even think to conquer.

She stood with her hands pressing at her temples as the shadow stooped to retrieve the soaked bundle of trousers. Then a haunting, eerie voice floated through the dawn as he walked off the other way. 'And shoot that damned dog!'

Verna looked down through the mist of her tears to where Sheba sat, tongue lolling over ivory fangs and dark brown eyes smiling up at her, and couldn't help but laugh.

'You traitorous, rotten little bitch,' she said to the smiling animal. 'You're nothing but a brazen, two-timing little hussy. Watchdog—huh! That man could have raped me, you know? And you, stupid, you'd likely have bitten *me* for resisting!'

Sheba flung back her handsome head in agreement and lifted one sandy forepaw for Verna to shake. She had liked the man, that much was obvious.

And Verna, on the other hand, hadn't even really seen him. If I met him on the street, wearing clothes, I don't suppose I'd even recognise him, she mused as she strolled on trembling legs toward her snug little beach house.

She'd know his voice, though, if she only heard it whispering into her ear. Or shouting at her across the water in the darkness. But would she recognise it in normal conversation?

Rare, he'd said. Cherish it. So why did she feel so terribly, horribly empty? He could have taken her, and Verna had no doubts about that. Dog or no dog he could have taken her, virginity and all. And she'd have helped him.

But he wanted her to cherish something that *he* had rejected. Something so rare he didn't want it at all.

Verna puzzled about it all the way home, unable to work out why she should feel so mixed up, so pleasantly buoyant and ... cherished ... and yet so lost and lonely and some-how unworthy. She puzzled it through her shower, and when she inspected her body with a new awareness and curiosity after it. She ate her breakfast with a splendid appetite and a glow that surged throughout her body. But when she dressed for work and struggled to pile her shin-ing, red-gold hair into a manageable knot on top of her head, she felt angry and dismayed and hurt.

'You can just stay in the yard and be thankful I don't lock you in the shed!' she swore at the excited, laughing dog that suddenly began to whine at the reality of being left behind. 'You're nothing but a traitor ... a two-timing little traitor!'

It took Verna only a few minutes to drive from her little rented house at Bargara into downtown Bundaberg, but once she'd parked her Mini in the slot allocated her behind the newspaper offices, she felt suddenly loath to step inside. She looked at her watch, discovered she had fifteen minutes in hand anyway, and walked slowly down Targo Street to where it intersected Bourbong Street, the city's main shop-ping artery.

She stood quietly at the corner in front of the bank, idly watching the passing pedestrians. Several quite acceptable young men eyed their way up and down her slim but shapely figure, and she wasn't unaware of the interest.

But her eyes were consciously seeking a particular coffee shade of hair—and a body she had memorised with her own even without seeing the face and those lips that had burned with a strange, compelling fire. And while it seemed as if every second man on the streets of the sugar city had hair of almost the right colour, not one of them looked at her with eyes that she knew must hold a special, knowing glitter.

Verna closed her own eyes momentarily, reliving the

touch of those lips and the feel of the iron arms around her body, then opened them again to reel with surprise at the shop sign across the corner from her. The Muscular Arm, it declared in blatant lettering, with a massive, flexing biceps and a clenched fist to prove the point.

Verna couldn't hold back the peal of laughter that burst from her still throbbing lips. The sign was so vivid, so ludicrous after her morning's adventure, that she could hardly accept its reality. And flexing her own arm in derogatory imitation, she turned on her heel and strode off to begin her first day's work. Her time for romantic dreaming was over; what lay ahead would be hard work and plenty of it.

She hadn't come to Bundaberg to find a man, but to get away from one, and even with the taste of the stranger on her lips, she couldn't ignore the bitterness of Stephen's betrayal.

CHAPTER TWO

THERE was no time during the next working week for day-dreaming of any kind. Verna spent her days in a frenzied whirlwind of activity, tying up loose ends with the outgoing editor and conferring with the paper's publisher on the varied editorial changes and layout alterations that would accompany her official take-over the following week.

Reg Williamson, the publisher, was a delightful man to work for. Verna took to him on sight, instantly reassured by his twinkling blue eyes and a chubby, almost cherubic appearance and manner. By the end of that first week she knew the job was going to be even more enjoyable than she'd imagined, since she was being given complete autonomy within a fairly broad set of general guidelines.

Circulation wasn't a problem, since the paper was a free weekly, distributed to each household in the city by mail. But advertising revenue could certainly be improved, and both Verna and Reg Williamson felt that a complete change in layout and story styles might help.

'It's not going to be an easy task,' he told her right from the start. 'But nobody's expecting miracles and we've plenty of time. A really fresh outlook will make a fair bit of difference, and I've got one more ace up my sleeve, if I can just arrange it properly. You've heard of Con Bradley, the novelist, I suppose?'

'Only by reputation,' Verna replied. 'I'm afraid I wouldn't be classed among his greatest fans. I tend to prefer somewhat tamer reading, myself.'

'Well, don't tell him that, for goodness' sake,' said Reg Williamson. 'If he agrees to write these columns for us, it'll be a fantastic booster, especially since he's said it would cost us only expenses.'

'It sounds great; what's the catch?' Verna asked, judging from the expression on the publisher's face that there would indeed be some kind of catch to the proposed arrangement.

'Oh, there's no real ... um ... catch,' Reg Williamson replied just a shade too quickly. 'Con and I are old mates, you see. We worked together in Canberra at one stage, and then again in Brisbane. Before he gave up journalism and started writing books.'

It was too smooth, and Verna's suspicions were immediately roused. 'There's something you're not telling me,' she said quietly, determined to get her new job off to a proper start by having all the cards on the table right from the beginning.

'Oh, nothing serious, nothing serious at all. It's just that I've sort of promised him total editorial freedom if he agrees to write the column,' Reg said with a slightly sheepish grin.

'What do you mean, sort of promised?' Verna demanded, automatically sceptical about any arrangement that would directly affect her own position and the demands upon it.

Reg shrugged. 'He wants to write it his own style and his own way. Con is an independent sort, and he's not exactly enamoured of editors ...'

'And especially not female editors—is that what you're getting at?'

'Oh no! Nothing was ever said about that. It's just that ... well, you've seen the paper as it is. Well, Con has too, and he sort of suggested that he hoped the new editor would be a pretty big improvement over the one you're replacing. There's nothing chauvinistic about it or anything.'

'Well, I certainly hope I'm some improvement, if you

don't mind me saying so,' said Verna. 'I'm sure that's one of the reasons you hired me in the first place.'

'Well, of course,' Reg said brightly. 'And I just know that you and Con will hit it off splendidly. He's a real professional, and he's been an editor himself, so there's no reason why you shouldn't get on well together.'

'It doesn't really matter how we get on, if he's to have total editorial control over his column,' Verna replied somewhat sarcastically. It was clear that Reg Williamson didn't relish the situation any more than she herself, but had been talked into it by his friend and was now committed.

During the rest of that first week, she was far too busy to worry about the potential problems of her new restaurant columnist, but it was never far from her mind, and when she was summoned to Reg Williamson's office the next Monday morning, it took little imagination to expect that Con Bradley and his column would have something to do with it.

'I hope you're free for dinner tonight,' Reg began without preliminaries. 'We're meeting Con to thrash out the final details on this column.'

'I suppose I can make time; I'll just have to,' she replied casually. 'Are we going to start it this week, then?'

'No ... it isn't quite that firm yet. Con says he'd like to meet you first, and if you can get together on the thing he'll do the first one for next week's paper.'

'You're taking an awful chance,' she grinned wryly. 'If he finds out I don't fancy his books, he just might refuse to write the column at all.'

'Then don't mention your opinion,' said Reg. 'I'm not asking you to pander to him, but I have to say that it's rather important to my ... our ... future plans that we get the benefit of his generosity.'

Verna waved her hands in a placating gesture. 'I have the message. I shall be nice as pie,' she said.

'Great! I knew I could count on you,' said the publisher. 'And please understand, Verna ... I'm not in the habit of taking away powers from my editors. This is a very special case, and not something you're going to have to be concerned about in general terms. No fears that I'll be asking you to play stories up or down because of advertising pressure or anything. Matter of fact,' he grinned, 'if Con still has his old newspaper style you might be glad to have him taking full responsibility for the column. He's liable to ruffle a few feathers around the town before he's done.'

'Just so long as I don't have to clip *his* wings,' she said soberly, then laughed aloud as Reg Williamson caught her word-play and grinned.

'I don't think you'll have any problems with old Con at all,' he said. 'He's got quite an eye for the ladies, unless he's changed a lot in the last few years, but what he likes best of all is word games. I reckon he'd rather argue than eat, so with your looks and your fast quips, he should be eating out of your hand. Anyway, I'll pick you up at seven, if that's okay. We're meeting him at the Don Pancho.'

He watched as she walked to the door, then called after her. 'Oh, and wear something ... you know, impressive. I mean, you always look very nice, but ...'

'I know; he's got an eye for the ladies,' Verna replied. 'Too bad I'm more interested in the food.'

'You mean you're not looking for a husband?' Reg Williamson's voice sounded so terribly sincere that Verna had to look round before she caught the gleam in his blue eyes.

'No,' she said, 'I'm not. So just stop your fancy match-making ideas, because if that's part of the game you'll lose both your columnist and your editor, I warn you.'

Reg raised both palms in mock surrender. 'Okay, you win,' he chuckled. 'But don't come to me if you change your mind after you meet Con. He's a handsome devil, and rich into the bargain.'

'And he's got editorial control. I'm not getting mixed up with any man I can't control,' she grinned in return. 'Besides, why should I need a handsome restaurant writer? I've already got a handsome publisher who's nice and safe and married, just the way I like 'em.'

'Ah, flattery will get you anything,' said Reg. 'If I was twenty years younger you wouldn't dare say things like that, but don't stop now; I like it.'

'Just practising so that I can charm the famous Mr Bradley tonight,' Verna replied. 'If he's really both handsome and rich, I might just have to use all my maidenly charms to keep him from taking over my job.'

'It's not your job you've got to worry about,' said Reg Williamson, suddenly serious. 'Just get him to write that column for us.'

Verna was conscious of the importance as she dressed for her dinner date that evening, but she was torn between a desire to please the nicest boss she'd ever had and her instinctive wariness of any columnist who could demand editorial freedom and get it.

She chose a close-fitting halter-neck in rich jersey, hoping the restaurant would be cooler than the summer temperatures outside. Her first few pay cheques would be going towards a new wardrobe, and it would have to be mostly cottons, she thought. Synthetics just couldn't stand up against cotton or wool in temperatures that regularly bounced over thirty degrees.

She chatted gaily with Reg Williamson during the brief drive from her small beach house to the Don Pancho Motel, and it wasn't until it began to appear that Con Bradley would be late that Verna's own nervousness started to grow with the passing minutes.

'I really am a little worried he'll decide not to like me,' she confided. 'This really is important to you, and I'd hate to be the one to mess it up.'

'Of course he'll like you,' the publisher laughed. 'My dear girl, I couldn't imagine anybody *not* liking you.'

'Oh, I know at least one enemy I've made already up here,' said Verna, reaching out to sip at her first Bargara Bomb, a potent concoction of orange juice and specially mixed liquors.

They were sitting in the small cocktail bar of the restaurant, and Verna thought Reg Williamson would fall off his bar stool, the way he laughed when she told him of her early-morning beach adventure. Of course she didn't mention the aftermath of the affair, but she told him about Sheba's trouser theft and her own teasing of their owner, embellishing the tale as she went along to increase her own bravado and the dawn stranger's boorishness.

'And I'll bet he doesn't go around skinny-dipping for a long time to come,' she said in conclusion, 'which serves him right, as far as I'm concerned. He deserved exactly what he got.'

'I wonder if his side of the story would be quite so amusing.' A voice like rumbling surf from behind them made Verna and Reg Williamson turn in unison.

'Con! How long have you been here?' the publisher cried with obvious delight.

'Long enough to hear most of Miss Grant's amusing little tale,' was the reply. 'I didn't want to interrupt her in the middle of it.'

Verna said nothing, her eyes locked with those of the tall, deep-voiced man before her. His eyes were like chips of ice, so pale a blue that they seemed almost colourless against the deep tan of his handsome features. Con Bradley was dressed in a light tan suit that set off his height and carriage magnificently, but it was his hair that caught Verna's imagination first.

It was over-long and shaggy, but it exactly matched her memory of that fateful morning on the beach, and she looked again at his eyes for some clue about her suspicions. But his pale, pale eyes were expressionless; only the slightly mocking sneer on his sensuous lips told her anything at all, and that was nowhere near enough.

As if sensing the immediate antagonism between his editor and his potential columnist, Reg Williamson leapt from his stool to perform the introductions, and then immediately suggested they move to their table. It wasn't until they were seated with fresh drinks before them that Con Bradley spoke again; his reactions to the introduction had been a cold, very formal nod and a disdaining glance.

'Sorry I was so late, old friend,' he said, eyes only for Reg Williamson. 'I got a phone call just as I was about to leave, and I couldn't avoid the delay.'

'Not to worry; you're here now,' said Reg. 'How's your work going, O.K.?'

'Slow but sure ... slow but sure. Always like that at the beginning, though. It'll pick up in time.'

'And have you ... er ... given some more thought to this column business?' Reg Williamson wasn't wasting any time, Verna thought, glancing quickly to Con Bradley as she tried to gauge his reaction.

The tall man's pale eyes flickered over to meet her own with an expression so chilling that she flinched before pulling her own gaze away, but when he spoke it was in warm, friendly tones.

'Always in a hurry, Reg! You really haven't changed since you moved to Queensland,' he chuckled. 'No patience at all!'

'Well, I just thought that ...' Reg Williamson was nonplussèd by Con Bradley's attitude.

'... that I'd take one look at Miss Grant's feminine charms and be instantly smitten, no doubt,' came the rumbling interjection. 'Not as easy as that, old mate, especially having heard her rather savage little story. I'm not at all sure I want to get tangled up with a paper that's edited by a veritable dragon.'

'Oh ... but I'm not ...' Verna caught herself before anything else slipped out. She'd already decided to try and let the men work out the problem for themselves, without getting any more involved than she had to.

'Not a dragon?' Con Bradley asked with a visible sneer. 'You wander around the beaches in the middle of the night, stealing the clothes from a poor, helpless swimmer and then taunting the poor fellow about it—and you want me to believe you're really just a sweet young thing at heart? Come now, Miss Grant, naïve I may be, but I'm not stupid.'

'But that has nothing to do with my capabilities as an editor,' Verna replied hotly. 'And besides, I didn't steal his pants, my dog did, and you can't really blame her too much; she's young, and not really very well trained yet.'

'I see,' was the rumbled reply. 'And tell me, Miss Grant, do you know the first—and golden—rule of dog training?'

Verna's mind raced through the host of dog obedience and training guides she'd read since acquiring Sheba, but no obvious answer came to mind and after a moment's consideration with both men eyeing her expectantly, she finally admitted, 'There's nothing specific that springs to mind,' hating herself for the tone of uncertainty that she couldn't keep out of her voice.

Con Bradley stared silently at her for a moment, and she knew he was deliberately building up the suspense for a line that would provoke a reaction. Finally he spoke.

'The very first thing to understand,' he said very quietly, 'is that you have to be smarter than the dog.'

Verna felt the blush creeping over her in the silence that followed, and was glad for the dim lights of the restaurant even as she knew that Con Bradley was quite aware of her discomfort. It was a struggle then to meet his chilling eyes, but she mastered the attempt and kept her voice as calm as possible when she answered.

'I'll try and remember that, Mr Bradley,' she said, and was rewarded with a wry grin of acceptance.

Luckily, the waitress arrived then to take their orders, and by the time that was over the moment of tenseness had passed.

The meal passed swiftly then, with the two men mostly reminiscing about old times and deliberately, at least on Con Bradley's part, avoiding discussion of the real purpose of their meeting. Verna was content to sit and listen, evaluating her potential columnist's table manners, which were excellent, and his knowledge of cuisine and wines, which was equally so. It wasn't until the coffee and liqueurs arrived that the possible restaurant column came to the forefront of the conversation again.

'What do you think of this column proposal, Miss Grant?'

Con's rumbling question caught Verna unprepared, since it became the first time he'd spoken directly to her since the meal had begun.

'I think it has very great potential, if you handle it right,' she said honestly enough. 'But I can't really judge without seeing a sample, can I?' Then, before he could answer, she continued almost spitefully, 'And of course my opinion isn't worth much, since you're to have total freedom from my editorial interference.'

'I gather you don't agree with that,' he said, and raised

one dark eyebrow in amusement at her obvious search for
the right words to answer with.

Verna took a deep breath, aiming to control the strength
of feelings he was rousing by his haughty, scornful attitude,
and she tried desperately to keep in mind Reg Williamson's
plea for co-operation. But it was no use.

'Not in principle, no,' she said. 'As editor I'm responsible
for style, and for the legal implications of anything in my
paper. I don't fancy giving any of that responsibility away.
And certainly not just to pander to some hot-shot writer's
ego.'

To her surprise, Con Bradley smiled broadly for the first
time that evening, a wide, happy grin that seemed to light
up his entire face.

'And so you shouldn't,' he said seriously. 'An editor has
to be God, or next thing to it. I always was when I played
at it, and so did you, Reg,' he added, turning to his friend
with another grin. 'However, we can't always have everything we want, can we? And I don't fancy some editorial
dragon playing power games with my own deathless prose,
regardless of the principle involved.'

He was being deliberately sarcastic about it, but the point
was being made and Verna felt her heart sink at the obvious
outcome of his determination.

'Well, it doesn't matter what I think, anyway,' she said.
'You have your promise from Mr Williamson, so I'll just
have to go along with it.'

'Why? You could always resign in protest.' Con's icy
blue eyes were calmly chilling, and he ignored Reg's immediate cry of protest, locking his glance with Verna's as
he waited for her reply.

'I could, but I won't,' she said with equal calm. 'Al-
thought I reserve the right to change my mind after I've

seen your work. If you agree to write us the column, that is.'

'Oh, I'm going to write it,' Con assured her, and she saw Reg slump with relief. 'In fact, I'm even prepared to suggest a compromise, which might just surprise you.'

Verna's expression made any denial ridiculous, so she dropped her gaze and muttered, 'I wouldn't have thought you to be much of a man for compromises, Mr Bradley.'

Her answer was another of those vivid grins; he had her on the run and he knew it. 'And I'd have thought you might be a shade more gracious than that, Miss Grant,' he said. 'Or are you only gracious in victory?' It was a deliberate innuendo about her beach escapade, but Verna resolved not to rise to the bait.

'Perhaps after I've heard your terms, I shall be,' she said gracefully.

'Right! In deference to your principles, which I applaud, I accept that you must have the right to edit for style. And of course you must take legalities into account, although I'm certain we'll have no problems there in any event. But I insist that responsibility for content is mine and mine alone. After the first few efforts I'll manage to conform pretty well to your style anyway, so all we have to quibble about is length, since I'd rather not see this type of column chopped about simply for space reasons, except in an emergency, of course.'

Verna was aghast. It was so totally reasonable a proposal, especially in view of his implied rigidity, that she couldn't find words to express herself. Reg Williamson was positively bubbling in his relief at the easy compromise, but Con Bradley merely stared deep into Verna's eyes as he awaited her response.

'I ... er ... I ...' She was stammering and she knew it, but she simply couldn't get the words out properly.

'Just say thank you, Con,' he prompted with a ghost of a grin.

'Th-thank you, Mr Bradley,' she replied.

He shook his head in mock anger. 'Thank you, *Con*,' he corrected her.

'Thank you ... Con,' she replied somewhat sheepishly, eyes downcast at the flurry of emotion that suddenly coursed through her body.

'You're welcome ... Verna,' he replied gravely, and she raised her eyes to meet a mocking, boisterous grin that for once extended even to his eyes. 'You'll have the first column tomorrow night, if that's early enough for us to start this week.'

'Afternoon,' she replied. 'Four o'clock deadline, and even that's stretching things as I'll have to rearrange things considerably. But we can always wait and start it next week.'

'No, let's start now,' he replied, and Reg Williamson nodded agreement. 'Noon, then, which should give you plenty of time. And for the future, let's look at first thing Monday morning as a deadline, although I'll try to get a couple of weeks ahead of the game.'

'Thank you,' said Verna. 'That would make it a great deal easier all round.'

'Well, I'm glad that's settled,' said Reg Williamson. 'And now I think I'll consider getting home. That's if you're ready, Verna?'

'Oh, no. You, my friend, shall first buy a bottle of champagne for us to toast this agreement,' said Con. 'And decent champagne, mind you, none of this lolly water they sell to the peasants.'

Reg's unhidden discomfort was a surprise to Verna, but the surprise was quickly dispelled by Con Bradley.

'Ah, I can see I'll have to fill you in on our friendly publisher here,' he said to her. 'Never, never, never take money with you when he invites you to dinner, or lunch, or even when it's just for a beer—or you'll end up paying for the lot. Our Mr Williamson is so cheap he squeaks when he walks.'

It was a brand of irreverence that shocked Verna just a bit, especially with the object of the assault sitting right beside her, but Reg took it all in his stride, treating the matter as a joke.

'But I thought you invited us for dinner, Con,' he objected. 'I mean, I'd have brought more money otherwise, but in the circumstance ...'

'... it's lovely they accept credit cards, isn't it, old mate,' Con interjected without turning a hair. Then he signalled the waitress over and ordered the champagne before anybody could think to object.

'And give the whole bill to my father, here,' he told the startled waitress, grinning at the laughter that exploded from Verna at Williamson's expression. Then all three of them were giggling happily, and Verna realised she'd just witnessed two very good friends playing a game that was all their own.

They were still chuckling when the champagne arrived, and Con took over the conversation.

'Verna's story reminds me of one I think you might enjoy almost as well,' he said, speaking directly to Reg Williamson but keeping his eyes fixed upon Verna, who was sipping at her champagne. 'It's about this girl I knew —or almost knew, if you take the Biblical connotation. She had a dog named Sheba too. Strange animal it was; she called it a Boxador, but not as strange as the girl herself. Do you know, of all the unlikely things you'd ever expect, she was a ...'

The reality of it struck Verna like a blow to the stomach, and as the blood drained from her face, she dropped her

champagne glass from nerveless fingers to splash the liquid
down the front of her dress before it tinkled off the edge of
the table and landed with a dull thunk on the carpet.

How *could* he? Her mind flew into a maelstrom of mixed
emotions, the most obvious being sheer terror. She wanted
only to flee, but in the instant of silence as both men turned
to look at her, she felt as if she were bound to the chair. She
couldn't move, couldn't think, couldn't speak. Only sit like
an executioner's victim and await the axe.

'... journalist like you, Verna,' Con's words echoed un-
really in her mind. She couldn't at first believe what she'd
heard.

He'd continued speaking as if the glass-dropping incident
hadn't occurred, but his eyes flickered with sardonic
laughter as he leaned over with apparent concern. 'Goodness, dear girl, you've gone all white and ... strange,' he said
worriedly. 'And you've dropped your glass. Did I say something to upset you?'

She shook her head mutely, unable to meet his eyes and
afraid to speak lest she break into uncontrollable hysterics.
She heard Con turn to assure Reg Williamson that she
would be all right, only affected by the champagne, he suspected.

'You're sure you're all right, Verna?' Reg asked solemnly,
and she had to look up and assure the publisher that yes,
she was fine, really.

'Just somebody walking over my grave,' she said in shaking tones. 'I'm sorry, I don't know what came over me, but
I'm all right now.'

Con had waved to the waitress for a fresh glass, and as
Verna held it in trembling fingers he reached out to close
his fingers over hers as he poured. His touch was like a
brand, sending shivers of emotion through her body until

she felt brittle as crystal, brittle—and likely to shatter at any instant.

Finally she forced herself to look up, expecting ... what? Surely some expression, some clue in those horrid icy eyes, but there was nothing.

In fact Con didn't even seek to hold her glance, but turned to Reg Williamson and began yet another story, apparently oblivious to the fact that he hadn't finished the first. Verna was secretly grateful, as it gave her some opportunity to regain her composure even if it did nothing for her whirling brain.

She couldn't help but look at him, evaluating his coffee-coloured hair, his height and regal, muscular bearing. Could this tall, pale-eyed man really be the naked stranger she'd dared to taunt on a lonely beach? Or was her conscience playing tricks on her, leaving her vulnerable and over sensitive to his words? Surely, she thought, his deliberate tale had been more than idle coincidence. She had been so certain, so positive, that he'd end his sentence with the words 'twenty-eight-year-old virgin' that she'd heard them drumming through her brain despite what he'd really said.

And Con Bradley knew it. Or did he? All of Verna's years of journalistic experience had taught her that truth sometimes *is* stranger than fiction, but this incident was too vivid, too close to home. She continued to look at him, drinking in his features, memorising them despite her fervent prayer that all this really *was* a coincidence, until she suddenly realised he was returning her appraisal.

His eyes caught hers, holding them by the vivid strength of his will, and for a moment it was as if they were alone in the room. Then the eyes shifted, moving across her face on an exploration of their own, boldly taking in her individual features before moving casually down the slender column of her neck and across her bare shoulders. It was as if his fingers, not his eyes alone, were caressing her, and Verna could literally feel his touch. The eyes moved lower, burning through the clinging material of the halter-neck to bring her breasts to rigid attention.

She was mesmerised, totally unaware of anything but the power in those eyes as they stripped away her clothing and laid bare her every defence. She felt like a slave on the auction block.

Then his eyes returned to her face, and to her horrified surprise, Con dropped one eyelid in a broad, deliberate wink. And as she sat, open-mouthed and staring, he began to speak.

'I'm sorry if that story I was going to tell earlier upset you, Verna,' he said very gently. 'It *was* something I said that upset you, I gather?'

Something you didn't say, but of course she didn't dare say it. Or admit it. 'Oh no, it was just something—something I thought of,' she replied hurriedly. 'Not your fault at all. My imagination just got away from me.'

It was a patently flimsy explanation, and Verna couldn't meet his eyes as she delivered it and hoped he'd let the matter drop. But no such luck.

'Well, you shouldn't think of things like that,' he said in that low, gentle tone. 'I've never seen anybody go all strange like that before. I thought you were about to faint or something. And you're still pale; you look like a sacrificial virgin ... about to go under the knife.'

His final words rang hollowly into her ears as Verna lifted her head to meet the expression in his eyes. And this time she wasn't disappointed. There was a joyful, triumphant mockery there, a jeering laughter that fairly shouted out his victory. And it was all she needed to have her humiliation complete.

For a second her mind simply went blank, and when it

leaped back into gear there was blind, naked anger in her own eyes. But she kept it out of her voice when she replied softly. 'At any age, Mr Bradley?'

'Why not?' His voice cut her off like a knife. 'After all, you're only ... what? ... twenty-eight. That clinched it, and Verna felt herself grow rigid as she fought for control. Her nails dug into her palms like daggers and her eyes flashed as she threw back her head and stared into his laughing eyes.

She knew in her mind that Con Bradley would have his revenge now, and it would be a revenge far outweighing the severity of her offence. Simply by telling Reg Williamson the true details of their encounter on the beach, he would ensure that it would be all over town by the time a day had passed. Reg was a sweetie and a dear, but he was a chauvinist beyond redemption and an even worse gossip; he would never be able to resist repeating the story in every humiliating detail. Verna closed her eyes for a brief instant before turning her attention to the publisher, morbidly eager to see the expression on his face when Con finally ended her torture.

'But maybe you're right,' said the rumbling voice. 'Anyway, virgins at any age are boring.' And then, to Verna's surprise, he changed the subject entirely and soon had Reg Williamson off on a long-winded reminiscence about their days together in Canberra.

The flood of relief that flowed through Verna left her so weak that she feared for an instant to try and leave her chair, but leave it she must. And finally she managed the strength to totter off to the powder room, where she stared into a mirror at the face of a pale, haunted stranger. She thought for a moment she was going to be sick, but that, too, passed, and finally she was left with no alternative but to return to the table and pray that her reprieve was more than just another twist of Con's torturing sense of humour.

She took no further part in the conversation, but couldn't help listening to every word Con said. And the more she tried to convince herself she was safe once again, the more she found herself flinching every time he started a new sentence, and every time he looked at her. But gradually she fell under the spell of his deep, resonant voice, and her mind slid away from her conscious control to return once again to the deserted, moonlit beach where that same voice had drummed through her ears to touch her very soul.

Only this time the shadowy figure that emerged from the sea had a face, a face with ice-like eyes and a wide, lovely smile that revealed white, even teeth. A strong, rugged face, with two fine creases across the broad forehead, and little laugh wrinkles around the eyes. The faintest suggestion of a dimple creased one cheek, and there was a slight cleft in the strong, determined chin.

She felt again the power in those massive hands as they locked her body against his, and that very power brought with it a sense of comfort when he said things like 'rare' and 'cherish'. But then the eyes changed to pale slivers and the mouth curled into a sneer around the words 'too rare for me'. Then mocking, horrible laughter thundered in her ears, and she heard, over and over and over, 'Virgins at any age are boring.' It repeated itself over again and again, and the lights before her eyes whirled like a kaleidoscope.

Then a hand like a branding iron clamped on to her own, and she heard a voice saying, 'Verna ... Verna!'

Dazed, she opened her eyes to find Con Bradley staring at her with what seemed to be a real concern in his eyes, though even as she watched his expression changed to a sort of wry humour.

'You're really going to have to stop doing this,' he warned. 'I know old journos' reminiscences are boring stuff, but it's no excuse for having nightmares at the dinner table.' He held on to her hand even when she tried to free it, and the sheer force of his will brought her out of her reverie and into the present.

'I'm ... I'm sorry,' she said haltingly. 'I don't know what's the matter with me. Perhaps I'm overtired or something, but I really think I should call it a night.'

Reg Williamson rose to his feet and also declared his intentions of leaving, saying he'd drive Verna home whenever she was ready.

'No, really it's all right,' she said. 'You two just carry on, and I'll walk home, if you don't mind. It's not very far, and I really feel that I could use some fresh air.'

Reg looked sceptical, but Con Bradley said, 'Yes, that's the way I feel too. I'll walk along with you, Verna. It's a bit late to be roaming around without your faithful guard dog for protection.'

'Oh ... no, please ...' Verna protested. The absolutely last thing on earth she wanted was to be anywhere with this man, and most especially not alone.

'Don't be silly.' He ignored her continued protest and took her gently by the arm, waving a casual goodnight to the publisher as Reg Williamson went off to straighten out the account.

Once down the steps to the motel complex's beach-front, however, Con immediately released Verna, seemingly content to stroll silently beside her as they went along. Only when her high heels threatened to bog down in the soft sand did he again take her arm, but only to steady her.

Nonetheless, his presence was like a pall on the quiet and solitude of the beach, and Verna felt like some sort of prisoner on exercise parade. Her head was clearing in the light sea breeze, but inside she was still writhing in the torment of understanding the degree of power Con Bradley now held over her.

She stopped. 'Please,' she said. 'I can go the rest of the way by myself. And I really would rather be alone.'

Con ignored her for a moment, then turned with a grin. 'But surely you're not going to deny me the chance to meet your infamous canine companion Sheba? I've been looking forward to it all evening.'

It was an unlikely comment, and Verna couldn't help but reply. 'Oh, for God's sake stop it!' she cried. 'You've already ...'

The look on his face stopped her. It was a bland, calm glance of real confusion, or at least it appeared to be. 'What *are* you on about?' he asked. Almost believable.

'You know very well what I'm on about,' Verna replied angrily.

'But I don't, I assure you,' he said quite calmly. 'Really, Verna, do you think that I'd *lie* to my *editor*?' There was just enough sarcasm in the question that she was forced to stop once more and peer up into his icy blue eyes. Could she be imagining it? No, there was just too much coincidence involved.

'I think you'd lie to your own mother, if it suited you,' she replied, turning away from him abruptly.

'Only if it was for her own good,' he grinned. 'And white lies don't count.'

'Well, then you'd lie to me, too, if you thought it was necessary,' she charged.

'Of course.' Such a bland admission did nothing for her inner turmoil except to accentuate it. Verna had taken all of this that she intended to take.

'Well, it doesn't matter anyway,' she raged. 'I don't care any more if you tell the whole damned town!'

'Tell the whole town what?' His calmness was infuriating,

especially in light of her own lack of it.

'That ... that I'm a twenty-eight-year-old virgin!' There —she'd said it, and damn the man. He could broadcast it from the rooftops, for all she cared. At least it would be over then, and he would no longer have this incredible, frightening power over her.

'*Are* you?' Both his eyebrows rose in mock astonishment and his mouth formed an enormous O of apparent surprise. 'Well, fancy that!' He looked down at her with amusement clear across his handsome features. 'But why would I want to tell anybody?' he asked with wry seriousness. 'I mean, it wouldn't be a secret then, would it?'

'It's hardly a secret now, is it?' she cried, oblivious to the tears in her eyes until he reached out with one gentle finger to wipe them away.

One eyebrow was raised in studied casualness when he said, 'But that hardly answers my question.' Then his eyes roamed boldly over her face and figure with something of the intensity she'd felt in the restaurant. 'And what if you are?' he asked. 'It's obviously by choice rather than circumstance. Are you ashamed of it or something?'

'Of course I'm not ashamed of it! I just don't like being considered some kind of freak, that's all.' Her eyes blazed in the moonlight, and she had to forcibly restrain herself from reaching out to try and slap away his insufferable calmness and control.

'But I don't consider you a freak. Why should I want to do that?' His voice rumbled softly against her ears, and Verna felt herself growing closer to sheer hysteria at this gentle, probing torture.

'Of course you do,' she snapped. 'All men do ...'

She paused abruptly as his huge hand reached out to capture her wrist and hold her still. His eyes blazed with an inner fire she couldn't read, and she could see the trembling of his strong jaw muscles.

'Let's get one thing straight right now,' he growled. 'I am not *all men*. I am me! And I'd be a helluva lot happier if you'd judge me by my own actions and not anybody else's. And I have never considered you a freak.'

Abruptly he released her, and Verna almost stumbled with the violence of his release.

'Well, it's the same thing,' she muttered to herself, hearing once again those horrible words *too rare for me*.

And suddenly she was terribly weary of the whole thing, weary of it and heartily sick of playing his silly game. She stopped in her tracks, only partially aware that they had reached the track that would take them away from the beach and up towards her small house.

'Look! Let's just quit playing this stupid game,' she cried. 'I know and you know that it was you on the beach the other morning, and we both know that I didn't tell Mr Williamson *everything* that happened, so you can just quit playing innocent.'

To her surprise, Con Bradley chuckled out loud and flashed her a broad grin. 'My, this just gets more and more interesting,' he said in a smarmy voice. 'Tell me, just what *did* happen during your little dawn raid?'

'You know damned well what happened!'

'Well, then, it won't hurt you to tell me your version,' he said placidly. 'There are two sides to every story, as you should very well know. Besides, I'm intrigued at why you're so positive that I'm the fellow whose pants you stole. I recall quite distinctly that you told Reg you'd never seen his face and wouldn't know him again if you met him in your soup.'

'Oh, come on.' Verna replied scornfully. 'You don't expect me to swallow that garbage about the girl you met with a dog named Sheba, and a Boxador as well. I may be ...

innocent, but I'm not totally gullible. You've been hinting at it all evening, taking cheap shots every chance you could get.'

'Sounds to me like a guilty conscience talking,' he replied with that disturbing calm. 'And you still haven't told me what I'm supposed to have done.'

'No, but I ... I ... I won't!' she decided suddenly, stricken by the vague possibility that she just might be wrong about all this. Could she be imagining Con Bradley's involvement? 'If it was you, you already know what happened, and if it wasn't, then it's none of your business anyway.'

'I'd say it's very much my business if I'm going to be blamed for it,' he retorted, taking her arm as he began to lead her up the narrow path. He was quiet until they had reached and crossed the road and Verna automatically turned towards the gate to her yard. At their arrival, a black shadow flew out to plaster itself against the gate, whining happily and thumping the fence with its tail.

'Ah, so this is the infamous Sheba, watchdog and stealer of trousers,' Con laughed, reaching down over the fence to stroke the wriggling animal. Then he opened the gate, handed Verna through it against the explosive flurry of leaping dog, and followed her into the yard.

'Come and let's have a look at you,' he murmured, and Sheba trotted obediently over to him, then flung herself down in a brazen plea to have her tummy rubbed.

The dog's reaction only served to make Verna even more angry, especially when she compared it to the dog's normal reserve with strangers. She had an almost overpowering urge to attack Con Bradley herself in hopes that the dog would join in, but somehow she knew it wouldn't work that way.

'Damn you, Sheba, you're supposed to take his leg off,

not beat him to death with your tail!' she snarled, and the black shadow grinned happily up at her before turning to continue licking at Con's hand.

'Nice to see somebody in the house likes me,' Con said drily, rising to tower over Verna. 'I don't suppose you're going to invite me in for a nightcap.'

Verna looked up at him, feeling her anger wash away in the bitter feeling of betrayal. Damn Sheba! Damn Con Bradley! She felt betrayed ... and worse. It was like the feeling of personal violation she'd felt on the single occasion in Melbourne when a burglar had broken into her flat and vandalised what he didn't steal.

'Well, I'll be off then, now that you're safe home,' he said unexpectedly. 'Good night, pretty girl.'

Sheba whined softly at his abrupt leavetaking, and Con was striding swiftly down the road before Verna realised she didn't know if he'd said good night to herself or to the dog.

'And I damned well don't care, either,' she whispered, although she stood watching his tall, long-legged figure until it was out of sight.

He never had admitted his presence on the beach, she thought after she had undressed and crawled into her bed. But it just had to have been him, no matter how much she wished it hadn't been.

Then, just as she was drifting off to sleep, she thought that if he'd kissed her on this night, she would have known. Only he hadn't, and somehow she was vaguely disappointed about that. Arrogant, hateful man! But handsome. And far, far too cunning.

CHAPTER THREE

VERNA was far too busy the following morning to concern herself with Con Bradley. She started the day with just the hint of a headache, but that soon disappeared under the pressures of her deadline, and by noon she had all of her pages away except the one she was holding open for Con's column.

And overall, she was rather pleased with *her* first edition of the paper, in that it was a better laid out and more informative production than those of her predecessor that she'd seen. Page 2 had a picture of her supposedly assuming command, and although she felt slightly embarrassed at that, preferring to shy away from the limelight, she realised it was necessary. And at least it was a flattering picture.

Her two young journalists, Dave Burgess and Jennifer Cox, had already shown themselves to be both eager and talented, so when noon arrived Verna announced a small celebration and took them off for a Chinese luncheon.

She'd left on her desk the logo that would head up Con's restaurant column, a stylised formal bib, bow tie and monocle with the caption 'Bib'n'Tucker' blazoned on the front of the bib. It was, she'd decided, quite a nifty little production, and a note pinned to it on her return seemed to agree.

'I like it,' the note said quite simply, and beside it was an envelope containing the first instalment of the controversial restaurant column. Verna's first reaction was one of pleasure. He'd liked her logo. But an instant later she was angry with him again because she didn't really care if he liked it or not. Savagely, she ripped open the envelope and began to read.

He was a craftsman; under any other circumstances she'd have given him that much. But her reaction as her eyes flew over the words started with anger and quickly sped through frustration, horror, despair and finally sheer blind rage as she read the column through once, and then again.

She was oblivious to her surroundings, unaware that the blood had drained from her face to leave her with a haunting, deathlike pallor. And that her two young journalists were sitting and staring at her in genuine shock at this transformation from the pleasant, happy lady who'd bought them lunch and complimented their work.

All Verna could see were the words before her, words that cleverly—oh, so cleverly—portrayed her as 'Dragon Lady the Editor', a snaggle-toothed, sulphur-breathing, fire-snorting apparition without a single redeeming feature.

Fairly shaking with anger, she read it through for a third time, seeing how Con Bradley had managed to sing the praises of the Don Pancho restaurant and its excellent food, which he had apparently enjoyed while in the company of a female monster that ate children for dessert, turned recalcitrant wine waiters into cane toads, and herself had worse table manners than her thieving, mischievous black canine 'familiar'.

Verna closed her eyes after the third reading, as if that alone would change the typescript. Her fingers clenched as if to crush the paper, then flew up as if to rend it into shreds. She flung it down in disgust and sat, eyes closed and breath coming in great, heaving sobs, then just as quickly she leaped to her feet, grabbing up the copy as she dashed from the room.

Reg Williamson looked up in startled amazement as she flung open the door to his office, marched in and flung the column down on his desk with a gesture of disgust.

'I will not have this garbage in my paper,' she cried. 'I will not! And I don't care if you do fire me. I'll quit before I'll run that!'

'Hang on, hang on,' he said soothingly. 'What's all this, anyway?'

'It's the so-called restaurant column that your great mate Con Bradley expects me to put in this week's paper, that's what,' she shrieked. 'And I won't ... I won't!'

She was pacing back and forth in front of his desk, almost tearing at her hair in frustrated rage, when Reg said, 'Damn it, sit down, girl. Give me a minute to read this before you start screaming again.'

Chastened, but in no way mollified, Verna perched on the edge of a chair as Reg Williamson leaned back in his huge office chair and began to read. She kept her eyes on his cherubic face, staring as if she could, witch-like, influence his reaction to the column.

And to her absolute horror, she first saw his eyebrows raise in token amusement, then there was a grin, and then a genuine belly-laugh that continued throughout the rest of his reading. He finished with tears streaming down his cheeks and his voice ragged from the laughter.

'Oh ... oh, it's beautiful. Absolutely beautiful,' he chortled. 'Oh, my very word! Oh yes, we'll drag in the restaurant ads with his kind of stuff.'

'But ... I ... we ...' Verna was stuttering and speechless with emotion. 'You don't actually expect me to run that rubbish?'

Williamson looked at her with honest bewilderment on his face. 'But of course,' he said. 'It's *fantastic* copy. Your first edition will be talk of the town an hour after it's on the street.'

'But ...'

'Oh, come on, Verna. You're not taking this personally, are you? It's a gimmick ... and a damned good one at that. Where's your sense of humour girl? I mean, I'll admit it's a little bit pointed, but even *you* must admit it's damned funny.'

'I don't admit any such thing,' she retorted angrily. 'It's crude, clumsy, vicious and not in the least bit funny. And I'm not having it in my paper!'

'Of course you are,' Reg said placidly. 'You're just upset at the moment, that's all. By tomorrow you'll realise just how *good* it really is, and you'll think differently. I mean, you can't expect the readers to take it seriously, not with that lovely photo of you on page 2. How did you ever get this far in the business if you're that over-sensitive?'

'I am not over-sensitive; I'm disgusted. And all right, this week there's the picture to offset Con Bradley's so-called sense of humour. I'm not planning on running my picture every week just to do that.'

'And I'm sure he's not planning to make you a regular feature in his column, either,' Reg Williamson said calmly. 'Now why don't you go and get this stuff set and into the page? I'm really quite busy just now, and I haven't got the time to keep discussing it.'

'You're insisting that I use it, then?'

'I'm *advising* that you use it,' he said with quite unexpected coolness, 'because it's damn good stuff—and because I'm certain you're a good enough journalist to realise that, once you put aside your personal feelings about it and start looking at it professionally.'

It might not have been a deliberate choice of words, but it was the right one. If there was one thing Verna did take pride in, it was her professionalism.

Stung by the publisher's implied criticism, she grabbed up the copy for the column and fled from the room almost

in a panic, cursing Con Bradley under her breath as she
stormed back to her own office.

Her frustrations were only increased when she found
that Con had—miraculously—matched her own standards
of style so well that there wasn't a single word she could
change in the editing of the column. Not one! She was so
thoroughly disgusted by the time she'd finished with the
page layout that she considered for a moment tearing up
her carefully-drawn logo and substituting something else,
but then she realised the author of the despicable column
would know her displeasure, and probably relish the evidence. So she pinned the logo carefully to the copy and sent
it all off to be prepared.

Then, pleading a headache, she went off to have some
coffee and try and soothe her shattered composure.

The paper was well and truly put to bed by the time
Verna left for home that afternoon, and clearly the Bib'n'-
Tucker column had already been circulated throughout the
building. As she walked through on her way to the parking
lot, she could feel the stares and hear the giggles as the rest
of the staff laughed at her.

And seeing it actually in print the next day didn't help
matters. Both Dave and Jennifer made an admirable
attempt to restrain their own laughter when they read the
column, but they were too young to do it well, and certainly not well enough to hide it from Verna.

'I suppose you two think it's absolutely hilarious?' she
demanded in a fit of pique that left both of them staring at
their desks with hangdog expressions and down-cast eyes.
It was Jennifer, slightly the bolder of the two, who finally
looked up and said, 'It is, actually.'

Their sheepish expressions quickly melted Verna's anger,
at least at them, and she found herself smiling her response.
'I suppose so,' she said, 'but when I get my hands on Mr

Con Bradley he won't think it's so smart . . . or funny.'

But she didn't get a chance to do anything with Con Bradley, because he neither telephoned nor visited the office personally. Which didn't surprise Verna one bit.

And certainly she didn't need his presence to be reminded of him. Wherever she went in the building, it was to a chorus of jokes and smart remarks about Dragon Lady the Editor, as the various staff members did their own research into the new editor's sense of humour.

She knew that if she let them get her goat she'd be branded something even worse than Con Bradley's portrait, so she tossed back smart cracks of her own and laughed right along with the others. But even so, it was a joke that quickly palled, and before the day was out she had lost all sense of humour about the situation.

When Reg Williamson poked his nose into her office and made his own contribution to the hazing, she snapped back with a threat to turn him into a cane toad, and everybody could see by the fire in her eyes that she wasn't kidding.

By the following morning, a Thursday, the worst of it was over, and Verna's temper had cooled to the degree that she graciously accepted a luncheon offer from Garry Fisher, the advertising manager, even when he'd prefaced it with a sly dig at her new title.

Garry was a tall, ascetic-looking young man who looked far more like a scholar than a hard-bitten ad salesman, but he had a hard-sell reputation that was quickly borne out by the results he achieved, and Verna knew he was highly regarded in the town.

He was clearly well known at the restaurant he took her to, and they were greeted effusively by the proprietor and his wife. The friendly greeting put Verna quite at ease, until Garry introduced her.

The proprietor nodded wisely and said, 'Ah, the Dragon

Lady,' and his wife nodded agreement and looked at Verna as if she expected her to bite.

It got even worse when they sat down and ordered. A group of little old ladies across the room were chatting happily until one of them whispered something to the others and fumbled around to get her copy of the paper from her bulging handbag. Verna wouldn't have noticed, except that their whispers were over-loud, perhaps because they were all hard of hearing, and the entire restaurant heard the smallest and sweetest-looking of the old girls saying, 'But she doesn't look like a dragon.'

Pride kept Verna from leaping out of her seat and fleeing the scene. Pride, and the look of genuine joy on Garry's face. He looked as if he'd like nothing better than to see her personally boost her outrageous reputation, even as he whispered, 'You're going to be famous, love. Give it another fortnight with that column and you'll have your own fan club—and I'll have restaurant ads coming out of my ears.'

'Well, don't hold your breath,' she snapped. 'Because I have no intention of ever being so much as in the same room as Con Bradley, let alone eating with him!'

'Oh, don't be so touchy,' he replied. 'Be honest, he's got the paper to where it'll be the talk of the town, and *you* get all the credit. Nothing the matter with that, love; if it was me, I'd be offering to buy him lunch once a week.'

'And you're welcome to him. Personally I don't need to make myself a laughing stock just to sell newspapers. And I'd rather starve than give him another chance to ridicule me in my own paper!'

The food arrived then, and conversation ceased as they dug in. It wasn't until Verna had taken the first few bites of a rather pleasant prawn cocktail that she suddenly realised it wasn't only their own conversation that had stopped, but almost everybody else's as well. Glancing obliquely

from the corner of her eye, she realised with growing horror
that *everybody* was watching her.

'For God's sake, do they expect me to gobble it up like a
dog, or what?' she hissed at Garry, who was obviously enjoying his own plate of oysters mornay.

'Probably,' he replied with studied nonchalance. 'People
tend to believe exactly what they read in the paper—you
should know that. Maybe if you put the dish on the floor ...'

Verna's vengeful glare cut him off in mid-sentence, and
he looked uncomfortably down at his food before resuming.
'I'm sorry; that was a bit much. Would you like to go?'

'Not on your nelly,' she muttered through clenched
teeth. 'That would really do it up right. No, I shall stay and
see it through, using my very best manners if you please.
And to hell with the lot of them!'

'Good girl! Never let the bastards get you down, I always say.'

But it was easier said than done. Verna used her very best
table manners, as promised, but they couldn't compensate
for fingers that trembled and a mouth that somehow moved
just as the forkful of food reached it, or the wine glass that
was slippery as quicksilver.

She struggled through it, but by the end of the meal she'd
dropped her fork twice, spilled gravy and wine both down
the front of a new and expensive blouse, almost choked to
death when a piece of fish went down the wrong way, and
had spilled salt all over the table cloth.

Worse, she knew that everybody in the place had ob-
served and recorded each incident in glowing detail, and
that she'd be the chief topic of conversation around dozens
of dinner tables that evening. By the time she returned to
her own office, she looked a total mess and felt like going
off to hide somewhere. Faced with strange looks from Dave
and Jennifer, she angrily shooed them off to find some

'decent stories for a change,' then slammed the office door shut, flung herself face-down on her desk, and cried her heart out.

Twenty minutes later, her eyes swollen from weeping and her humiliation and anger condensed to a knot of white-hot rage in her stomach, she opened up the door again and returned to work. And she worked with a vengeance, driving herself and her staff throughout the rest of the week to the point where her Dragon Lady image became all too real inside the office.

And at home, where her 'black familiar' took the brunt of Verna's bad temper, the atmosphere was equally chilly as Verna plotted revenge after revenge upon Con Bradley.

The following Monday she was back to normal, breezing into the office with a cheerful smile for everyone and even congratulations to Jennifer for her work on a particularly difficult story. Until noon. Or more correctly one p.m., when Verna returned from lunch to find Jennifer sitting at her desk with a look of rapture on her face.

'Mr Bradley was here,' she breathed dreamily. 'He left you a note. Gee, I don't see why you hate him so much, he's so handsome, and ... and ... well, *everything*!'

'When you get to be my age, dear child, you'll realise that being handsome means nothing at all,' said Verna, feeling somewhat like a maiden aunt to the young journalist who was an exceptionally innocent twenty years of age.

Seating herself at her own desk, she picked up the note, read, 'Hoped to take you to lunch, but you'd gone,' and crumpled the paper to throw it angrily into the waste-bin.

'I'd starve first ... or poison your soup,' she muttered angrily, then ripped open the other envelope to scan over Con's restaurant column for that week. She could feel Jennifer's eyes on her as she read it with growing anger and amazement, and she wasn't surprised when the younger girl flinched with alarm as Verna flung the copy down on the desk and swore, 'Bastard ... bastard ... bastard!'

She was halfway to Reg Williamson's office, the copy in her trembling fingers, when she realised he was off to Brisbane for the day, and she turned back to her own office with a mumbled curse.

Seated once again at her desk, she read over the column again, debating with herself if she actually dared throw it away.

The content of this second instalment centred this time around the very restaurant where Verna had endured her luncheon fiasco of the previous Thursday, was no worse than the first column. Only this time she was reported to have impaled olives on her talons, snorted candles alight from across the room, decried the lack of flying fox on the menu, and eaten a steak so rare that it kept jumping off the plate. Worse, he'd somehow heard of her wine-spilling and gravy-dripping accomplishments and had included them, as well.

'Can I read it, please?' Jennifer asked meekly from across the room.

'What?' Verna roared her question at the girl, who looked down at her desk with the suggestion of a tear in the corner of her eye.

'I only want to read it,' she said quietly, and then, with astonishing and somewhat indignant anger, 'I know you don't like it, but I expect I'll find it quite funny, and I don't see why I shouldn't read it.'

The look in Jennifer's eyes brought Verna down to earth rather quickly, and she scolded herself for taking her own bad temper out on Jennifer. It wasn't Jennifer's fault that Con Bradley had this astounding power to shred Verna's feelings like so much cabbage.

'Of course you may read it,' Verna said gently, rising to pass the offensive copy over to Jennifer. Then she returned to her desk and got busy laying out her final pages, trying to avoid watching Jennifer's reaction to the column.

A difficult task, not only because she was sub-consciously aware of the girl's interest in the column, but because Jennifer made no attempt to hide her amusement. Like Reg Williamson the week before, she was giggling helplessly by the time she'd finished.

Then she brought the copy back to Verna, and said with a perfectly straight face, 'The lobster dish sounded quite tasty.'

Verna looked up to meet huge, soft brown eyes that fairly danced with compassion, and found her own anger incapable of resisting. As Jennifer's mouth twitched with the attempt to keep a straight face, Verna felt her own mouth begin to quiver as well, and seconds later they were both howling with laughter.

'But he'll pay for this,' Verna vowed through tears of laughter. 'I don't know how, but I'll make him pay if it's the last thing I ever do. The swine! I should go to lunch with him if he asks me, just so I could poison him, or slip hot peppers into his beef stroganoff or something.'

'Well, don't do anything too drastic,' said Garry Fisher's voice from the doorway. 'He's managed to triple our rest-aurant advertising this week, and I've already more en-quiries about next week. You're going to have to boost it to twenty-four pages next week, if this is any indication.'

'You're joking!' Verna didn't—couldn't—want to be-lieve that much success for the column.

'I never joke about money,' he said very coldly, and the super-serious expression on his face made Verna want to start giggling all over again.

'All right,' she said, 'but if I don't get this final page laid out, you'll have a late paper on your hands, and your advertisers won't like that.'

'*Our* advertisers,' he said pointedly, turning to leave the room.

Verna stuck her tongue out at his retreating back, causing a spate of giggling from Jennifer, then sat down to the serious business of wrapping up the paper for another week. It was just on five o'clock when she finished, and despite the air-conditioning she was hot and exhausted.

'I feel like a limp dishrag,' she said to Jennifer, who was clearing away her desk in preparation to go home.

'Me too. A beer would sure go down right,' said the young journalist. 'What do you reckon?'

'I reckon that's a terrific idea,' Verna replied honestly. 'But only one, because I've got a hungry dog waiting at home.'

In actual fact, they had two each and Verna quite enjoyed the break, despite one of the tape operators greeting her with a shout of 'Yea, Dragon Lady,' when they entered the pub.

That evening she took Sheba on a lengthy stroll down the beach, consciously avoiding the area where she had encountered Con Bradley—or had she?—on that fateful morning that seemed like only yesterday. And she did the same during the next few nights and the one early morning when she rose early enough for a stroll. Then she decided it was silly to avoid the area, since the sheer fact of avoiding it made her think about Con and their first meeting anyway.

'And besides,' she told herself in the mirror after suddenly bouncing into wide-awake energy at three-thirty in the morning on Sunday after a boring, boring Saturday night at home, 'it's bad enough he slanders me in my own newspaper, without dictating where I can walk on the public beaches!'

And having said it, she dragged Sheba out of a sound sleep, snapped on the dog's leash, and deliberately set off for that memorable stretch of Kelly's Beach.

'And I hope you *are* there, Con Bradley,' she said out loud. 'Because I'll not only steal your trousers, but everything else you could use to cover yourself as well. And if you just dare come out of the water after me again, I'll throw rocks at you!'

By the time she reached the spot of that first encounter, she had worked herself into such a state of nervousness and anger that even Sheba was growling at every passing shadow, but the display of ferocity was quite wasted, since there was nothing but shadows to appreciate it.

Verna stayed in the area, watching the sun rise up out of the ocean in a beautiful, dreamlike sunrise, and felt strangely lonely and disappointed when she walked back along the beach behind the fleeting black shape of her dog.

Stripping off shorts and T-shirt, she plunged into the shower after giving Sheba her breakfast, and luxuriated in a leisurely shower and shampoo before wandering out into the kitchen. Wrapped only in a towel that barely concealed her slender body, she was busy breaking eggs into the frying pan when a rap on the kitchen door made her turn in surprise.

There was the briefest impression of a face looking through the screen at her before Verna realised that her towel was slipping, and she clasped at it frantically as she dashed for the bedroom. Even as she shrugged into clean shorts and a tank-top, fumbling in her haste, she couldn't believe what her eyes had told her, until she returned to the kitchen and flung open the door.

'What the hell are you doing here?' she demanded in her most authoritative voice.

Eyes like chips of ice stared blandly back at her, and Con

Bradley reached down to scratch Sheba's back before he answered her.

'Well, it's a good thing I didn't come for breakfast, because your eggs are burning,' he said with a slight grin, and Verna turned round and dashed back to rescue them, aware that he had followed her into the room.

'You get out of here!' She was shrieking like a fishwife and she knew it, but she didn't care. And obviously neither did he. He stood leaning casually against the refrigerator and watched her scraping hopelessly at the charred eggs.

'It would probably help if you turned the heat off under them,' he said calmly, and with tears of rage in her eyes, Verna turned around with the pan in her hand to fling at him. Only her wrist was caught in a grip of iron as he stepped forward in a single cat-like stride, and halted her.

'Naughty, naughty,' he said, shaking his head reprovingly. 'Just think of the mess you'd have to clean up if you missed. Even Sheba wouldn't eat that muck.'

Verna made another attempt to free her hand, and when Con merely grinned at her, she reached out with the other hand and grappled for the kettle on the other burner. But it was futile; Con merely reached out and captured that hand as well, which only brought her closer to him as he held her with arms wide spread.

'Now settle down,' he said softly, although Verna could feel the steel in his voice. 'This is a helluva way to treat a man who comes to offer you a drive in the country and lunch as well.'

'Lunch!' The word emerged as a childish squeak that only fanned Verna's anger. 'I wouldn't have lunch with you if ... if ...'

'If you were starving, I suppose,' he grinned. 'And I suppose it's all because of this column business, which I must say you're taking extremely calmly.'

'You let go of me and you'll soon see how calm I am!' she raged, struggling against his grip and wondering if she dared use her knee against his unprotected groin.

'I wouldn't try that,' he said as if reading her mind. 'Fun and games is one thing, but that just might make me angry.' And then, to her absolute amazement, he let go both her hands at once and stepped lithely back out of immediate striking distance.

'What are you *doing* here?' she asked again, her voice lifting with each word until it was little more than a squeal at the end of the question.

Con shrugged casually. 'I just happened to spot you on the beach and followed you home,' he said. 'What were you doing down there—looking for your naked stranger, or just more trousers to steal?'

It was too close to home, and Verna's mouth shut with a clunk, cutting off her retort. She stared up at him coldly, then turned away and flung the frying pan into the sink. 'None of your business,' she said childishly.

'Okay. How long will it take you to get ready to go for our drive?'

'You go to hell!'

'Only if we can get back by tomorrow morning. I've got next week's column to write.'

He didn't raise his voice, but stood there totally unruffled and apparently oblivious to Verna's flaming indignation.

'And I suppose that's why you're inviting me along,' she cried, 'so you can gather more ammunition. What's the matter ... can't you find enough things in your tiny little imagination?'

She'd turned to face him again, and despite the tears of anger in her own eyes, she was slightly taken aback at the sudden expression of seriousness that flashed across Con's face. But it only lasted an instant, before it was slowly replaced by one of total incredulity.

'Oh ... oh my God,' he murmured as if to himself. And then louder. 'Oh, come *on*; you're not taking this Dragon Lady the Editor thing *personally*?' That magic smile lit up his face as he moved closer to peer down into her flushed face. 'You are!' he cried with unstilted delight. 'You're actually taking it personally ... you think I'm out to get you.'

Verna stood there and watched his face dissolve with unsuppressed laughter, and just as he seemed about to collapse from it, she brought back her hand and smacked him across the cheek just as hard as she could manage it. The impact drove him hard against her refrigerator, and instantly changed his laughter to rigid, icy anger.

Gingerly, he reached up to touch his jaw, where the mark of her stinging fingers shone like a brand. Verna looked into those cold, cold eyes, and steeled herself for the blow she expected, but when he made no move to strike her, she followed hard on her earlier attack.

'And just what else *would* I think?' she screamed. 'How can I take it anything *but* personally, when you make me the laughing stock of the whole town? And don't you dare try and tell me it wasn't deliberate, Con Bradley, because I wouldn't believe you if you swore it on a stack of Bibles as high as you are. You deliberately set out to humiliate me, and you managed it, damn you, but I'll get even if it's the last thing I ever do!'

Her words flowed even more quickly than her tears, and soon she felt as though both would flood them right out of the kitchen, but Con just stood there, silently, looking at her.

'I don't suppose you'd accept that I thought up that approach before I ever even met you?' he asked. 'No, I didn't think you would.'

'Well, if you did that just makes it all the more despicable,' Verna raged. 'Because then it's just pure, chauvinist piggery, which is about what I'd expect from you anyway.'

'You really don't have much of a sense of humour, do you?' He stood there, looking at her with that infuriatingly placid calm, and asked the question almost as if he were speaking to himself.

'Sense of humour? I'll give you sense of humour!' Verna shouted, turning to grab at the first thing she could lay hands on to strike him with. Her fingers closed around something and she turned with it shining in her hand, striking blindly at the huge figure before her. Then it was as if she'd smashed her hand into a brick wall; her entire arm and fingers went rigid with pain and then a strange numbness, and she looked down at where the kitchen carving knife lay, still spinning slowly, on the floor beside them.

'Oh ... oh my God!' she whispered, stricken to the very soul by the seriousness of her attack. Her eyes flashed to meet his, then ran quickly over his body to see if she'd actually cut him. But she couldn't have ... wouldn't have, she thought. Would she? She raised her face to meet his blazing, cold eyes again, the words forming in her throat but strangling before she could get them out. 'I ... it's ... but ... I couldn't ...'

Con's eyes ranged across her figure, eyeing her with none of the passion she had seen in the restaurant and later on the beach. This time they held only a chill loathing, and she shivered under their icy stare.

His earlier stares had made her feel naked, vulnerable but at least desired. This time she felt like some tiny, insignificant reptile, or creepy crawling thing, and it seemed as if she would shrivel beneath the intensity of his gaze.

The silent appraisal went on for days, it seemed, and Verna stood there in total silence, shivering both from his disgust and from the nearness of what she had almost done. And from her own self-disgust, which threatened to shake her apart right before his eyes.

And then he spoke, in a voice that rumbled up like thunder from a grave.

'My God, but you take yourself seriously, don't you?' he said, shaking his head as if he couldn't quite believe it. Then he turned and walked to the door, shouldering it open as he turned and flayed her to the soul with one final comment.

'God! It's not much wonder you've kept your amateur status, with an attitude like that.'

And then he was gone, stalking past a wriggling Sheba with a soft, gentle pat on the tummy, and out to cross the street and drop out of sight towards the beach. He never once looked back, though Verna watched him as long as he was in sight.

CHAPTER FOUR

VERNA spent the rest of Sunday house cleaning, trying in vain to use physical effort as a weapon against her growing self-recriminations.

The very thought of her attempted attack on Con Bradley made her almost physically sick, and the wounds caused by his final, slashing remark were kept open by her own guilty conscience. The fact that his statement might have been wholly deserved did nothing to assuage the hurt, and Verna's feelings ranged from a tearful sorrow to a hot, blistering anger at the man who could strike such a blow to her self-esteem.

Monday morning dawned after a night in which she might as well not have bothered trying to sleep, and she stared aghast at the dark smudges under her eyes when she went to brush her teeth.

'You look like something the cat dragged in at midnight, old girl,' she muttered ruefully, and then moaned at the unexpected thought that Con Bradley had probably slept like the proverbial baby, despite the near-miss assault. He was just the type, she thought, so terribly calm and self-assured that even a hysterical woman with a knife couldn't disrupt his cool.

Getting through the morning's work was an ordeal; everything that could possibly go wrong, did.

'What you're seeing is "Verna's Law",' she told Jennifer at one point during the morning. 'What can go wrong, will; and what can't, we can arrange. It's days like this I wish

I'd got married at sixteen so I could let somebody else do the worrying.'

The two women slipped out for lunch, leaving Dave to mind the office. Technically, it should have been Verna's turn to sit out the lunch break, but Dave merely shrugged at her explanation of editor's privilege, saying he'd rather eat later himself anyway. Nothing was said about the real reason behind the switch—the fact that Verna couldn't possibly have survived it if she'd had to stay alone in the office and wait for Con's delivery of his column.

If he brought her a column at all, she thought during lunch. It would serve her right if he didn't, and Verna knew it, but her own assessment of Con as a professional made such a move highly unlikely. He wasn't the type to let personalities interfere to that degree with any agreement he'd made.

Nonetheless, Verna was vaguely surprised and tremendously relieved when she returned to the office to find the expected envelope waiting on her desk.

'Did he ... er ... say anything?' she asked Dave in as casual a voice as she could manage. Her stomach was all aquiver, expecting her young journalist to pass on some vivid and highly deserved message, but it was not to be.

'Nope,' was the equally casual reply, and Dave was off on his own lunch break without another word.

Verna was all too aware of her trembling fingers as she lifted the envelope and stared at it for some time before reaching for her letter-opener. Then the feel of the cold, blunt blade in her fingers threw up a vivid reminder of the morning before, and she laid both opener and envelope down on the desk as her stomach lurched.

She could feel the tears readying themselves, and blinked hastily, shaking her head in reproach at the surge of emotion she couldn't quite control. And when she finally ripped open the envelope and began to read that week's 'Bib'n'Tucker', she had only to skim through the first few paragraphs to feel herself trembling with even greater emotion.

Con Bradley might as well have slapped her face. The column made no reference to Dragon Lady the Editor; none at all. It was a straight, simple review of the chosen restaurant, devoid of humour, devoid of any sparkle, and so totally removed from what Verna knew her readers had already come to expect that even *she* felt mildly cheated.

The message was horribly, deliberately clear: You've made it clear enough now that you don't like *my* kind of column, so here it is—*your* way! And Verna could have wept at the coldness of it all.

It was, she realised, exactly what she deserved. And that realisation struck her like a physical attack that left livid spots of colour in her cheeks and a heartrending emptiness inside her. He had been right; she had been taking herself far too seriously. Behaving, in fact, with a juvenile selfishness that suddenly seemed terribly repugnant to her.

And with that realisation, she knew also that it was extremely important to her what Con Bradley thought of her as a professional. And as a woman, although she knew it was now too late for that to matter very much. He had clarified that feeling all too well after she had tried to attack him the day before.

'And he's right,' she muttered fiercely. 'You deserve everything he said, and more.' The low comment brought a quizzical look from Jennifer, who took one glance at Verna's flushed colouring and prudently looked down to her own work.

Verna picked up the column and read it through again, trembling with the abrupt realisation that she couldn't ... wouldn't ... dare to use it. It would be unfair to the restaurant, for starters, since despite the glowing descriptions of food and service it simply didn't have the brilliance of Con's earlier work. She flung it down on the desk again; she'd just have to ask him to rewrite it in his usual style.

Ask? The thought forced a brittle laugh of sheer terror from her throat. She'd have to do better than ask, she thought. Beg would be a better word. For an instant, the thought of begging Con Bradley for anything made her rigid with anger, but only for an instant. She was the one at fault, and there was no getting around it. She tried honestly to look at herself in Con Bradley's position, and shuddered at the reaction. Even begging wouldn't be enough, she thought, I'd tell him to go and jump off a cliff.

It took her fifteen minutes of concentrated preparation before she could muster the nerve to pick up the telephone and dial his number. And even when the telephone at the other end began to ring, she didn't know what she'd say when he answered. She had seldom done anything that required an apology during her life, and certainly nothing that required such an abject apology. She simply didn't know what to say.

A movement in the corner of her eye brought Jennifer's presence suddenly to the fore, and Verna slammed down the telephone in a panic. She just *couldn't* talk to Con with anybody else in the room, she realised. It would be hard enough in total privacy.

Jennifer gave her a rather strange look at being sent out for coffee so soon after lunch, but she went without any argument, and immediately the room was clear Verna slammed the door shut and reached again for the phone.

It would serve her right if he flatly refused to discuss it, she thought. Then the thought of having to explain the whole to Reg Williamson and—even worse—Garry Fisher, struck her, and Verna almost dropped the telephone in her rushing apprehension.

She would beg. She would get down on her hands and knees in the middle of the main street and beg, she thought. And her heart thudded louder and louder as the telephone began to ring. Once, twice, three times, four times, and she couldn't face any more. She dropped the receiver with a frightening feeling of relief. Even having to explain would be easier than having to face up to apologising to Con Bradley.

Unless, of course . . .

The thought was so outrageous that at first she mentally shook herself for even thinking it. But as the minutes passed, the ridiculousness of the idea was overshadowed by the slim possibility that it just might work. At least for this week. Dragging out her files, she clipped Con's first two columns and read them over thoroughly, looking at them for the first time through truly professional eyes and ignoring the personal reaction of her earlier readings.

Then she stuck the paper in her typewriter and set to work, flinching at first at the unaccustomed effort of the job, but gradually finding an unexpected pleasure in what she was doing.

When Jennifer returned with the coffee, Verna drank hers thankfully but without conscious consideration. Her mind was totally occupied in the job of trying to rewrite Con's column in his unique style. It took her most of the afternoon, using the specifics and facts from his original straight report and weaving in her own fantasy of a dragon lady that was even more horrendous than the one he'd created.

The first effort, she discarded. It was simply awful. The second was better, but she simply couldn't match his unusual style of putting words together. It wasn't until she hit on the idea of writing the column herself—as Dragon Lady the Editor—that everything seemed to flow together.

It began with an apology. She had inadvertently burned her poor columnist's fingers, she wrote, which ought to teach him to try and filch cane toad fillets from *her* private stock. Of course it meant he was unable to review their visit to Il Gambero, but instead of firing him, she was condescending to write the column for him.

And she did—in a style that portrayed herself as a sneaky, scheming, totally awful old witch, and her poor columnist as a sweet, innocent little fat fellow who was totally intimidated by her. She stole his trousers, filched his money and had her black 'familiar' bite him on the ankles. And that was on a good day.

Into the narrative she wove the delights of the huge oysters and superb fish dishes they had enjoyed, along with all the comments Con had originally made about the food, wines and service. The facts were his, but the rest of the column was her own—and to the reader it would appear an appropriate response to his earlier efforts.

Or would it? Verna tried her best to look at the job from as coldly a professional viewpoint as she could manage, but it was too close to her. The next step was obvious, but she felt strangely reticent when she passed it over to Jennifer and demanded an honest opinion.

It must have been obvious to the girl that something very weird was going on, but she coolly read through the column, chuckling happily at some of the better lines, before she returned it. Verna was slightly ashamed at the letdown she felt at noticing Jennifer hadn't as obviously enjoyed this column as much as the previous ones, but that feeling disappeared at the girl's first comments.

'You really must have done something awful to him,'

Jennifer said with unexpected candour. 'It's a rather neat way to apologise.'

Verna's heart sank. 'It can't be *that* obvious,' she said. 'Is it?'

Jennifer shrugged. 'Only to me, I reckon. And to him.'

'Well, I certainly hope so,' Verna sighed. 'I'm going to be in a lot of trouble if he doesn't accept it.'

Dave returned to the office then, and both girls dropped the discussion. Verna turned her attention to finishing off her page layouts, and before she realised it, five o'clock had arrived.

The next day was the usual rush to deadline, but Verna found time to implement another little touch to her carefully disguised apology. Working through her lunch break, she carefully drew a small figure of a rampant, fire-breathing dragon puffing clouds of smoke and flame at a little stick figure of a fleeing man. A female dragon, obviously, since she'd added a hair ribbon and tied it in a bow on the creature's crest. It took her only a few minutes to rearrange the page to accommodate the artwork at the bottom of the restaurant column, and when she was finished, Verna breathed a non-sulphurous sigh of honest relief.

Giving a quiet thanks to the wondrous versatility of offset printing methods, she finished off that final layout and treated both her young journalists to a beer when the day was over. Dave only stayed for the one, pleading a very heavy date, but Jennifer insisted on returning the shout, and Verna allowed herself a few relaxing moments to enjoy the younger girl's company. Sheba was safe enough in the high-fenced yard, and was hardly likely to starve to death if Verna was an hour later than usual.

The icy brew was a welcome relief after the closeness of the office, and Verna felt herself begin to unwind for the first time since her flaming encounter with Con Bradley.

Also, she quite liked young Jennifer, who displayed a wisdom and maturity that often belied her years.

But she wasn't ever going to be able to cope with the younger woman's exceptional candour, she felt, startled when Jennifer suddenly said, 'I'm glad you're going to make things up with Con Bradley. Was it something really horrible that you did to make him angry?'

Verna was stunned momentarily, unable to think of any reasonable answer and yet loath to bluntly dismiss the question as being none of Jennifer's business.

'Well ... yes, it was, I guess,' she finally said, hoping Jennifer would be kind enough to let the thing drop at that point.

'You don't want to tell me, do you?'

Verna shook her head with a slow smile. 'It's a little bit ... personal,' she replied.

'Then why this great *public* apology?' Jennifer seemed unmoved by the flush that her question raised on Verna's cheeks. 'Or isn't he talking to you at all?'

How true. And how impossible to answer in words alone, Verna thought. 'I just thought it would be ... easier ... this way,' was all she could think to reply.

'Well, I sure hope I'm smarter than that when I fall in love,' Jennifer said somewhat pensively, and Verna recoiled in surprise.

'But I'm not ... that's quite ridiculous, Jennifer,' she replied hastily.

'Okay,' the younger woman replied with careful indifference. 'Lord, look at the time! I'll be late for tea.'

And she leaped to her feet and rushed from the pub, leaving Verna with a half-finished beer and a kaleidoscope of thoughts that seemed to spin unending in her mind.

She couldn't possibly be in love with Con Bradley. That was the first impression, and it didn't last long. Quickly replacing it was the horrifying realisation that Verna *was* in love with Con. Either that, or so close as to make no difference at all.

She sat, staring into the amber liquid and trying to rationalise her feelings. Certainly her carefully written apology was no more than an honest attempt to show her admission that he'd been right about the column all along, she thought. But it couldn't be denied that what bothered her most wasn't his disapproval of her professional attitudes. That was deserved, but it was a secondary consideration.

What really hurt was his condemnation of her as a woman. And that credibility she'd destroyed irrevocably.

Verna thought about it all the way home, and long into the night as she tossed and turned in a restless half-sleep that brought her into Wednesday morning more tired than when she'd gone to bed.

Her apprehension about how Con would react to the interference with his column was overshadowed by her bitter realisation that she *did* love him, and that it wasn't going to do her a bit of good.

She picked up her copy of the paper on the way into the building, and upon reaching her desk she quickly skimmed through it, relieved that the 'Bib'n'Tucker' column was free of typographical errors, and that her dragon sketch looked quite appropriate to the text.

During the day, she was the subject of various smart remarks from staff throughout the building, and she managed to laugh and joke in return. She didn't care what anybody else thought of the column today; all that mattered was the reaction from its proper author, and every time her telephone rang she had to mentally prepare herself for his comments.

But Con didn't telephone her that day, nor the next or

the next or the next. And although she made a special point of being home throughout the weekend, dreaming he might possibly show up in person, he didn't do that either. By noon the next Monday, Verna was a nervous wreck. She'd left space for the column, but she had absolutely no idea whether she'd get another one or not, and she realised that she'd never be able to contrive one of her own without deliberately going out for dinner alone that night to get the information she'd need.

And as noon approached, she found herself admitting she simply didn't have the nerve to stay in the office through lunch and see if Con would deliver the copy she so desperately required. She couldn't face him, couldn't possibly meet those ice-chip eyes and feel her bones melt with the urge to throw herself into his arms.

At eleven forty-five, she fled the office and went to hide in the pub next door, ignoring the taunts of surprised workers from the back shop who had adjourned early for their own liquid lunches. It was all Verna could manage just to sit quietly and sip slowly at a cold beer while her mind imagined all sorts of horrible possibilities.

The easiest would be if he didn't bring her any copy at all. At least she could explain that to Reg Williamson and Garry Fisher. They wouldn't like it, but at least it would take the pressure off Verna herself for the moment. Admittedly, she'd have to explain to the publisher that it was her fault Con had given away the agreement, but she'd face that reality when it arrived. If Con provided another straight column, she didn't know what she'd do. She didn't think she had the nerve to try another rewrite.

'You can come back to the office now; he's been and gone,' said Jennifer's voice, and Verna turned to find her young journalist looking at her with undisguised amusement.

'He didn't say anything,' Jennifer replied to the unspoken question. 'But he looked sort of ... pleased with himself, I guess you'd say. Although maybe that's not such a crash-hot sign, from your viewpoint.'

Verna didn't answer as she strode swiftly back toward the office with Jennifer scurrying at her heels. Her one thought was to see what Con had written, despite her confessed fear that it wouldn't be guaranteed to please her.

Jennifer sat quietly at her own desk and watched as Verna ripped open the familiar envelope and began to read, her eyes racing over the page as her heart leaped with growing pleasure and amazement. She finished reading, laid the copy on the desk, then abruptly picked it up and read it again. It was still unbelievable.

Her columnist, typing, he said, with one finger that had healed so far, humbly begged forgiveness from Her Ladyship, then went on to make her sound even worse than ever. The activities of 'old-sulphur-snout' and 'brimstone-breath' while allegedly dining at the Regatta Room were enough, he said, to have her barred for ever from civilised eating establishments.

Even worse was his description of her 'jealous' assault on an exceptionally luscious waitress who dared to look upon the poor injured columnist with a glint of pleasant lust in her eye.

It was an awesome attack on Dragon Lady the Editor, and Verna loved it. She sighed with a relief she wouldn't have ever believed possible. Her public apology had been accepted. In public ... but what could she read into the fact that Con had deliberately avoided staying to face her on her return?

Nothing! She flogged herself mentally for even thinking of it. The first and most important step in the reconciliation had been accomplished, and Con's acceptance of her professional apology was enough. To expect more, or even think of it would only re-open the wounds, and Verna didn't think she could handle that.

If she could get through the next few months, reading his column every week and knowing he'd accepted that one apology, it would be enough. Even if she never saw him again, although the thought of that sent shivers of hurt through her system.

And yet, while she could apologise in print for her attitude towards his writing, she couldn't use her paper to do the same thing about her assault on his body. And she couldn't imagine herself being given the opportunity to do it in person, even if she could find the words.

'May I read it now?' Jennifer asked her cautiously, and Verna passed over the copy with a grin.

'You'll love this one,' she told the girl. 'Dragon Lady lives again, with a vengeance!' And when Jennifer laughed and chuckled her way through reading the column, Verna took an unexpected delight in sharing the younger girl's attitude of happiness.

She reached out to crumple the envelope and dispose of it, and thanked her lucky stars for whatever impulse caused her to peer inside before she did so. Because the column hadn't been alone in the envelope; another piece of paper had been tucked in with it, and Verna felt her heart give a curious little lurch as she eased her fingertips inside to free it.

What emerged was her own little dragon cartoon of the week before, but where her drawing had the little stick man fleeing for his life, this one had him with his arms clasped about the lady dragon's neck, obviously giving her a great smacking kiss.

Verna blushed with pleasure at the little shivers of anticipation that shot through her when she looked at the cartoon. Perhaps there was a chance after all that Con would accept all of her apologies, she thought, her heart racing feverishly at the possibility. Or was there some other message here? Shaking her head in fond comfort, she rejected that possibility in favour of the far more pleasant dream that maybe he didn't hate her after all.

She was quite unaware of the revealing look on her face when she showed the cartoon to Jennifer before adding it to the layout for that week's paper, but Verna wasn't quite so lost in her own happiness that she'd miss the girl's laughing response.

'I thought he looked awfully smug about something,' she said. 'And I'm glad for you, I really am. Only ... couldn't you two find an easier way of getting it together? This thing is starting to shape up like a mail-order romance, or something.'

Both of them laughed at the suggestion, but Verna's laugh was loudest of all. She didn't care *how* they got back on speaking terms, just so long as it happened.

Verna's mood of luxurious happiness lasted throughout that day and the next, but when she'd heard nothing more from Con by Wednesday, she began to find it difficult to maintain her buoyant spirits. Maybe he was waiting to see if she'd print the cartoon, she told herself. Or maybe he was just busy with his writing or something. But by Thursday even that excuse seemed terribly, frighteningly fragile.

She went through the weekend in a daze of mingled emotions, angry with herself, angry with him, sorry for herself and drowning in frustration. She haunted the beach where they'd first met, but to no avail. By Monday she was in a temper so foul even his expected column wouldn't be enough to snap her out of it.

Young Dave quite deliberately made himself scarce, chasing up all manner of nebulous sports stories in a bid to avoid the office, and Verna's temper, as much as he could. Jennifer was sneakier, but no less determined to resolve the problem, as Verna found before the morning was out.

It was Jennifer's turn once again to cope with the lunch-hour office duty, and when she left on an assignment at eleven, Jennifer promised to return in time to let Verna get away before noon. A false promise, Verna thought to herself as the minutes ticked away and she realised she'd be alone to face Con's arrival.

Alone. The thought of it terrified her. She could have faced meeting him again with Jennifer on hand, and had actually considered staying with that in mind, but to meet him alone suddenly seemed an impossible task. Gone was the loneliness and lovesick frustration that had made her wander the beaches all weekend; as noon drew closer she felt only a growing apprehension.

She felt the bustle of activity in the building as everybody went off to lunch, but instead of hunger she felt only a huge lump of dread in her stomach. The clock seemed to shift into slow motion, ticking over the minutes like hours as she sat silent, unable to work, unable even to read the paperback she kept in her desk for whatever spare minutes she had during the day.

Five past twelve; the clock must have stopped, she thought. Ten past; perhaps he wasn't coming after all. A quarter past; surely he wasn't coming. Twenty past; she was planning a suitable revenge on Jennifer, who would be certain to have an unshakeable excuse. And by twelve-thirty, Verna couldn't take any more. The phone hadn't rung, not a soul had come anywhere near the office, and she no longer cared about her rule that it shouldn't be un-attended during the lunch hour.

Grabbing up her handbag, she walked quickly around the desk and through the door, reaching behind her to grab at the doorhandle to close it after her. Head down, she was plunging forward when a pair of soft leather loafers appeared in her vision.

As she raised her eyes, slowly and with growing apprehension, she was conscious of the gleaming white stockings, the tanned, muscular legs merging into cream-coloured shorts and shirt, and finally the pale blue eyes that regarded her steadily but with an unreadable expression.

'Bit late for you to be going for lunch, isn't it?' rumbled that familiar deep voice. 'And leaving the place unattended as well?'

'No, not really ... Jennifer should have ...' Verna was stammering, quite unable to get her words together properly, when Con handed over his envelope.

Their fingers met as she reached out for it, and she instinctively recoiled from his touch as it seemed to burn right through her hand. The envelope fluttered to the floor, and Con dipped forward to retrieve it.

'Shall we try that again?' he asked with a droll grin, his eyes roving over her body with an easy familiarity that brought every nerve alive in Verna's slender figure.

Hastily, she took the envelope and laid it on her desk, then turned to face him again, hoping he couldn't see how much she was trembling.

'Thank you,' she said, and then fear took over again. 'I ... I really must go,' she blurted, shifting to try and pass where his tall frame blocked the doorway. Con didn't move.

'Aren't you even going to read it?' he said quietly.

'Oh, it'll be just fine, I'm sure,' she replied. 'Listen, I really must go. I'm late already.'

'Where are you headed?' He asked it gently, but the expression in his eyes told her he knew she was making excuses.

'To ... to the hairdresser,' she replied hastily, reaching

up to touch the knot of reddish-gold hair. 'I'm getting it cut, you see. It's much too long for this heat, I find.'

'Oh, come now. You can do better than that,' he grinned.

'What do you mean?' Verna knew very well what he meant, but she wasn't going to admit it. All she wanted was to get herself away from his demoralising presence, before she did or said something utterly stupid.

'I mean you're not getting your hair cut, and you know it as well as I do,' he replied. 'Why don't you just admit you're afraid to be alone with me—even in your *own* office —and be done with it?'

'I'm not afraid of you,' she lied. 'Why should I be?'

Con shrugged. 'I can't imagine,' he said. 'Why are you?' Then he grinned wolfishly. 'Wouldn't have anything to do with the fact that I might ask you to apologise personally, I suppose.'

'For what?' Verna tried to look highly indignant, and knew she was failing miserably.

'Oh, for rewriting my column, among other things, although I will admit you did a splendid job under the circumstances.' He paused, obviously waiting, and Verna finally nodded and whispered, 'Thank you.'

'And then of course there's the matter of trying to carve me up for dinner, or had you forgotten that?'

Forgotten! How could he possibly expect her to forget the most despicable act of her entire life? she wondered, trembling visibly at the memory.

'I hadn't forgotten, and yes, I am very sorry about it,' she said, and then wondered at how easily it came out.

'Good, because I haven't forgotten it either,' he replied grimly.

'Or forgiven,' she whispered, as much to herself as anything else. The chill in his pale eyes had suddenly unnerved her, and her legs began to tremble under her.

'Do you really think you deserve to be forgiven?' he asked, raising one dark eyebrow with the question.

'Probably not,' she whispered so softly that he didn't quite hear her.

'What?' His voice seemed to roar into her guilt-alerted ears.

'I said probably not,' she answered, more loudly this time.

'Awfully hard on yourself, aren't you? Or did you really *mean* to chop me up with that knife?'

'Of course not! I just grabbed the first thing I could lay my hands on and that ... it ...' Verna couldn't continue; the vision of herself laying about with the dangerous, shining blade reared up inside her like a spectre.

'Good thing it wasn't an axe, then, isn't it?' Con's eyes were flashing to match her own, but there was a glint of humour there.

'It certainly is,' Verna replied frankly, then fumbled to a halt, uncertain what else to say.

'What time's your appointment?'

The question took her totally by surprise, and she didn't even know what he was talking about. 'What appointment?' she asked wonderingly, then flushed with embarrassment as she realised how easily he'd tricked her.

'Just as well,' Con muttered almost to himself. 'Bad enough you've got to wear such lovely hair in such a frumpy damned style, without cutting it all off.' He reached out to brush his fingers against the top knot, and Verna shied away from his movement.

'Hmm, touchy, aren't we? I pity the hairdresser if you react that way,' he laughed. 'But seriously, you're not going to cut it?'

'Well, not today,' she admitted bashfully. 'But I have been thinking of it. It's awfully hot when it's this long.

Which is why I wear it in this *frumpy* style; it keeps if off my neck at least.'

Her brief flash of rebellion was wasted. Con just stood silently, toying with his fingers along the edges of her fringe. 'Don't cut it,' he said, very bluntly.

'I will if I choose,' Verna retorted, surprised at the harshness of his command.

Con's hand dropped to his side and he looked at her with a strange grin on his face. 'Your choice,' he shrugged, 'but I might not love you any more.'

That was far too close to the mark for Verna's taste, but she didn't dare let him see just how close. 'Hardly significant, if you'd only love me for my hair,' she retorted with a shake of her head. 'And besides, you might like me with it short. Maybe being cool and comfortable would improve my disposition.'

'I can't imagine anything doing that,' he replied with lifted eyebrows, 'although lunch might help. You *will* join me, I hope?'

Verna immediately began to phrase a careful reply about leaving the office unattended, then thought better of it as she realised how silly it would sound. Still, the thought of dining with this man gave her the cold shivers; he simply had too much power over her.

'Really I'd like to, but I'm afraid there isn't the time,' she replied gracefully. 'There's just so much to do on a Monday; I'll have to get your column edited, for one thing, and ...'

'I can take the hint,' he interrupted with a brusque gesture. 'So I'll get out of here and let you work. That way you'll have no excuse at all for not joining me for dinner.'

Verna started to object, but Con interrupted before she even began. 'And since it's the night before deadline you'll have to be home to bed early, which will suit me just fine,' he continued. 'I'll pick you up at six-thirty, which even gives you time to feed my favourite dog.'

And he turned on his heel and stalked off before Verna could say another word, greeting Jennifer with a cheerful remark as he passed her in the corridor.

'Well, that was certainly nice timing,' Verna remarked coldly as her young journalist walked into the office without the slightest trace of guilt in her eyes for being late.

'I got a really good story out of it,' was the casual reply, 'but it did take longer than I'd expected.' And then, with a frankly curious grin, 'How did you make out with Mr Bradley? Are you still talking to each other, or did you smother him in fire and brimstone as usual?'

'That is none of your business, young lady,' Verna replied in half-serious anger.

Jennifer merely shrugged and retired to her own desk, but when Verna caught herself whistling happily later that afternoon and looked up to see Jennifer hiding a secret smile, she just couldn't stay angry.

'If you must know, I'm going to dinner with him tonight,' she said, 'although he probably just wants fresh ammunition for his column.'

'You've got the name, you might as well enjoy some of the benefits,' replied Jennifer. 'Speaking of which, can I have a look at this week's column?'

Verna passed it over and watched as Jennifer giggled her way through the reading. 'He's easing up on you,' was the assessment. 'Better watch out it isn't a trap.'

CHAPTER FIVE

JENNIFER'S warning, even though Verna realised it had been issued in jest, stayed in her mind as she showered and prepared for the evening ahead.

Having no idea where they'd be going, she was at something of a loss about what she should wear for the occasion, but the casual attitude towards dress standards in the heat of a Queensland summer made the decision less difficult than it might have been.

'Better to be overdressed than underdressed,' she told herself, idly wishing her mother had provided platitudes that would cope so easily with the turmoil of emotions Verna was suffering.

Now that she and Con were back on speaking terms, the thought of dining with him seemed somehow far less frightening than it had only six hours before, but the fear had been replaced by a quite different form of apprehension.

Verna realised her susceptibility was vastly increased by the realisation that she was in love with the tall writer, and she was instinctively fearful of letting him realise the extent of the power he held.

But she also wanted a chance to redeem herself, and maybe, just maybe, let the relationship take a more pleasant turn.

Please, please, please ... just let us get through this evening without fighting, she thought, only too aware of how easily this pale-eyed man could strike sparks from her own fiery person. And strangely so, since in her own eyes Verna considered herself fairly placid and easygoing. Not a doormat by any means, but hardly the word-slanging, knife-wielding harridan she had become in Con's presence.

'It's all your fault, Sheba,' she muttered at the chocolate-coloured figure that sprawled across her bedroom doorway with long pink tongue lolling happily. 'If you'd left his trousers alone in the first place I wouldn't be in this pickle, and now that I've got half a chance of getting everything under control I suppose you'll decide to bite his leg after all.'

She was just adjusting the ties of the soft pink halter-neck she'd chosen when a soft knock at the kitchen door brought Sheba to her feet with a rumbling, deep-throated growl.

'This is *not* the time, stupid!' Verna cried as she tried to get past the bristling dog so she could answer the door. As she approached it, she couldn't help but wonder if may-be the dog had understood her, and she had to stifle a giggle at the thought of Con Bradley being savaged by a dog who'd refused in the past to even think of protecting Verna from him.

'What's so funny; is my tie crooked or something?' Con asked as he entered the house with a suspicious glance at the knife drawer. Sheba, fortunately, greeted him with her usual lack of restraint, and once satisfied that he smelled right the dog rolled over to have her tummy rubbed.

Verna chuckled louder as she explained, carefully choosing her words, and was rewarded by a grin of what might be called sceptical amusement.

'You wouldn't bite me, would you, old girl?' Con said to the rolling figure. 'You know how to keep a fellow happy without all this nonsense of trying to bring him down to your level, eh?'

Verna bit her tongue to keep back the sharp retort that

immediately sprang to mind. No, she thought. No fighting tonight, no matter what he says.

'I'm ready when you are,' she said instead, flashing Con her brightest smile as she picked up her evening bag. Looking at his immaculate pale blue safari suit, she was glad of her own choice in clothing and equally glad of the look he'd given her to show his approval.

As they drove back towards Bundaberg, Verna found her eyes drawn to the lights on top of the Hummock, the only hill in the immediate district of Bundaberg. She realised with momentary surprise that this was the first time she'd driven past the Hummock at night, when it seemed much higher than in daylight.

'I suppose you haven't even been up there for a look around?' Con's soft-voiced question startled Verna, mostly because of the uncanny way he seemed to have of reading her mind.

'No, I've hardly played tourist at all,' she replied.

Then she had to stifle a giggle as he began to relate the history of the Hummock in a deliberately put-on tourist guide voice.

'The Hummock is only three hundred and sixteen feet high, and it was once an active volcano,' he chanted in a high falsetto. 'It is because of the volcano that the land around Bundaberg is so extremely fertile. From the top of the Hummock, on a clear day, can be seen Childers and Hervey Bay to the south and south-west, and Burnett Heads and Bargara to the north and north-east. The Hummock is totally surrounded by fields of sugar cane, and during the cane firing season it is a most popular look out. On top of the Hummock is a memorial to Bundaberg's greatest airman, Bert Hinkler.'

'My, you do that well,' she said laughingly. 'Have you ever considered becoming a tourist guide?'

'Only on my most depressing days,' he replied with a grin. 'I only remembered that bit because I was so struck by an entire district venerating a tiddly little hill like that. The view's good, though, I must admit that; we'll stop on the way home if we're not too late.'

'I'd like that,' Verna replied honestly enough.

'You'll probably change your mind when I tell you it's rather popular as a passion pit,' Con laughed. 'Especially since that handbag's too small to hold your carving knife. Or have you got a smaller one for going out in public?'

Verna coloured at his bantering, wishing he'd abandon all mention of that particular incident for ever. But when she said so, he only laughed at her.

'Easy for you to say, it wasn't you that was almost cut off in the peak of your vibrant young manhood,' he said. 'But don't worry about it, you're perfectly free to argue with me any old time, just so long as you keep your hands in your pockets.'

'Perhaps it would be easier if we didn't argue at all,' Verna replied in what she hoped was a meek voice. *Anything*, she thought, if it would make him change the subject.

'Easier, but booorring,' he answered, drawing out the last word in a sing-song tone. 'And that's the one thing I could never accuse you of, being boring.'

'I suppose that's some kind of compliment,' Verna said quietly. 'Or is it?' She couldn't help but remember his comment that first time in the restaurant, nor could she still her traitorous tongue. 'Or didn't you mean it when you said virgins at any age are boring?'

'What do you think?' His mouth quirked into a wry smile, but he kept his eyes on the road ahead.

'I think you're evading the issue,' she said with a sudden determination. Gone was her promise to have a quiet, unaggressive evening, and she was glaring daggers at him, poised for a quick retaliation no matter what he replied.

'And I think some people have unhealthy obsessions about things that are their own business and nobody else's,' he replied calmly. 'You brought it up, not me; if you want to fight, fight with yourself.'

There was a long silence then, lasting until they'd passed through the outskirts of the city and turned past the massive brick structure of the East Water Tower. Con drove carefully, but Verna could see his anger in the tightly-bunched muscles of his jaw.

'I'm sorry,' she said finally. 'It was my fault for bringing it up.'

'Okay,' he replied, 'I'll forgive you this time.' Then, as if nothing had happened, he switched on his tourist guide voice again with a wave at the water tower.

'Built in 1902 at a cost of one thousand eight hundred and ninety-one pounds, fourteen shillings and sixpence,' he chanted. 'The tower is one hundred and twenty feet high, with a thirty-foot inside diameter and walls that taper from a thickness of four feet six inches to about one foot. An absolute masterpiece of bricklaying.'

'You're amazing,' Verna laughed. 'You made that up!'

'I did not!' Con managed to sound quite indignant at the suggestion. 'It's all perfectly true, according to the local tourist brochures. I'm a sucker for hoarding bits of totally irrelevant information.'

'It must come in handy sometimes—for your books, I mean,' Verna replied. 'Or don't you bother mixing facts with all the sin, sex and sadism?' She wondered immediately what had prompted such a provocative question, but to her great relief Con only laughed.

'That's what I like, another faithful fan,' he said. 'But if you don't mind, I'd rather not talk about work tonight;

both of us get enough of that during the day.'

Swivelling the car through the centre-parking section of Bourbong Street, he secured a parking slot squarely in front of a restaurant called the Peacock Garden.

'I'm quite looking forward to this; I'm told it has superb Chinese food,' he said, then walked around to hand Verna out of the car.

Inside, they discussed the menu only briefly before Verna admitted her limited knowledge of Chinese cuisine. 'I'll put myself entirely in your hands,' she said, and instantly regretted the extravagance when Con ordered a variety of dishes and then specified bowls and chopsticks.

'I don't know how to handle chopsticks,' she said, only to be told,

'There's only one way to learn. Don't worry, I won't let you starve to death.'

'Of course not, you'll just sit there and laugh at me all the way through dinner.' It was a snippish reply that Verna regretted, as usual, only after it was out.

Con raised one eyebrow and shook his head sadly. 'You really have a thing about being laughed at, dear girl. Makes me wonder how you ever came through the journalistic ranks in the first place, with such a poor sense of humour. Or is it only poor when the joke's on you?'

There was just enough seriousness in the remark that Verna was forced to take herself in hand. This would never do! It would be impossible to get through the evening if she bridled at his every remark. 'It's not poor at all, usually,' she replied. 'It must be that you and I have what's commonly called a personality clash.'

'Hah! Don't go trying to blame it on me,' he retorted. 'And it's not a personality clash—it's a guilt complex. That's what's the matter with you, Verna, you feel guilty because your little mongrel friend stole my pants, or so you *think*. And because you're convinced I'm holding your sexual secrets over your head like a headsman's axe.'

She didn't ... couldn't answer, only look down at the table and hope nobody in the restaurant could hear him.

'Come on, admit it,' he said, and Verna raised her face to meet a pair of icy blue eyes that seemed to scorch her very soul.

'Admit what?' she said demurely, stalling for time and knowing he understood that very well indeed.

'Well, for starters you might try admitting that you're only guessing when you accuse me of having been your naked fantasy figure on the beach,' he said chillingly.

'You've never denied it,' Verna replied hotly.

'Nor have I admitted it, you might remember that. Especially since you've already refused to tell me just what it was that I did—presuming it was me, of course—that's been upsetting you ever since. I find that quite unfair.'

'I've already told you ... if it was you then you already know, and if it wasn't, it's none of your business.'

'See, you're admitting you're not sure,' he retorted calmly. 'Which means you either wish it had been me—or you wish it hadn't. Which?'

There was just no way in the world Verna could answer that question, any more than she could bring herself to tell this infuriating man what really had happened on the beach that morning. What if it hadn't been him after all? 'But it was you, I know it was,' she muttered through clenched teeth.

'Well then, it won't hurt to tell me all about it,' Con replied, 'or would you rather deal with this other little matter first?'

'What other matter?' He'd lost her for an instant, but as soon as she'd asked, Verna regretted it.

'Why your little secret, of course. The little secret that

you told me, unasked and uninvited, after our first dinner together. Don't tell me you've forgotten it already?'

His grin was a clear invitation for Verna to blow her cool entirely, and he knew it. 'I would really like to know why you've got such an obsession about the whole thing in the first place,' he continued. 'It's perfectly obvious that it's a situation that exists by your own choice, and you must have had hundreds of opportunities to do something about it if you'd wanted to; you're a gorgeous woman, you're obviously a very passionate person, and when you get yourself in the right circumstances, with the right man, the problem will take care of itself.'

Verna had dropped her eyes to the tablecloth, but now she looked up to meet Con's own gaze, unsure just what expression she would find there. To her slight surprise, he was regarding her quite soberly, without even a hint of humour or ridicule in his eyes. And he'd called her gorgeous, passionate even! He *must* be laughing at her.

'I'm not, you know.' He said it very gently, and despite her immediate surge of anger at him reading her mind, she couldn't deny the honesty in his eyes. He *wasn't* laughing at her.

'I realise that,' she said. 'And I suppose I *am* overly defensive about it. It's just that ...'

Con's blue eyes took on a strange expression, one that seemed to act like a magnet that started the flow of her words. Hesitantly, at first, and then suddenly in a great rush of pent-up emotion and anger, she told him about Stephen, about her own feelings for a man who'd lied to her, cheated her, and finally ...

'He laughed at me,' she said bitterly, 'and it wasn't funny laughter; it was like somebody laughing at a cripple. And then he ... he offered to ... to fix it for me!'

Con's explosive oath was so foul that at first she didn't

believe her own ears, but the icy look in his eyes, the whiteness of his clenched fists on the table before her, suggested
she'd actually heard right. He looked away from her, and
she could sense his embarrassment, and knew somehow
that he wasn't embarrassed about what he'd said, but about
Stephen's actions.

'There are days I'm almost ashamed to be a man,' he said
then, so softly she could barely hear the words. His fingers
clenched and unclenched, and Verna could feel the table
vibrate with the tension inside him. Without thinking about
it, she reached over to take one of his fists in her own
slender fingers.

His eyes, like two pieces of flint, stared at her unseeing,
then gradually slid back into focus with a softness so warm,
so gentle, it took her breath away.

There was a moment, a moment a lifetime long, when it
seemed to Verna as if she and Con were the only people in
the entire world. She looked into his eyes and wanted to
drown there, aware that her own eyes were crying out her
love for him, and totally uncaring that he should hear that
cry. Then the waitress arrived with the first course of
their meal, and Verna could have shot the woman. Con's
eyes returned to normal, and he turned away almost
brusquely to order a bottle of wine before turning his
attention to the food.

'Okay,' he said to her in a voice she barely recognised.
'This stuff is chicken in rice paper, which probably isn't
the best dish for you to learn to handle chopsticks with, but
it's the best one to start a meal, far as I'm concerned.' Rising from his chair, he came around the table to stand behind
Verna using his huge hand to guide her movements as he
instructed her in the use of the curious instruments.

'The bottom one stays steady and you move the top one

against it,' he said, demonstrating with his own and gently manipulating her fingers until she began to get the feel of it. The mere touch of his fingers sent such shivers of absolute ecstasy through Verna that she could barely control her own fingers, then all too soon it was over.

'Don't worry about being a bit sloppy,' he grinned at her from across the table. 'I've already destroyed your table manners in print anyway, remember?'

'Well, even if you hadn't, I'd have done it myself before this meal was over,' she grinned back, dropping her portion of paper chicken for the third time just as it reached her mouth.

For some reason, she found the honey prawns easier to handle, although Con scowled at her when she tried to spear one on a chopstick instead of delicately picking it up as he did. The barbecued chunks of pork chop gave her a bit of trouble, since eating them involved holding the pieces in the chopsticks while she bit off a portion, and by the time she got round to trying the fried rice Verna was able to handle the chopsticks reasonably well.

'See, I told you it was easy,' Con smiled over the gradually diminishing pile of goodies before them. The waitress arrived to refill their wine glasses, and Con waited until she'd disappeared before lifting his glass in a toast.

'To Dragon Lady the Editor,' he said with a grin. And Verna was already raising her own glass when he continued, 'and may all her fantasies be fulfilled.'

If only he knew just what fantasies lurked behind her gracious smile, Verna thought, he'd probably be running for cover! 'And to her creator,' she replied, lifting her own glass.

To her surprise, a flicker of a frown crossed his eyes, but then he smiled and raised his own glass, silently.

Throughout the rest of the meal, Con seemed just a

touch reserved, as if his mind wasn't quite all there in the restaurant, but was partially off somewhere on a journey of its own. Several times Verna had to repeat herself because he missed what she'd said, and gradually she found it increasingly difficult to keep the conversation alive.

Her own imagination filled in the reasons quite well: obviously he had seen her look of undisguised love, and it was beginning to worry him. Because, of course, he didn't fancy any serious involvement with a girl whose innocence put such a distinct liability on the relationship. There had been, she was sure, many women in his life, women able to offer him physical satisfaction without the emotional implications Verna realised his knowledge of her own situation would involve. Well, fair enough, she thought. In a way she could hardly blame him. Only why did she have to love him? It's just not fair, she thought, and had to forcibly restrain herself from thumping the table and crying out her indignant anger.

When they finally left the restaurant and began the silent drive back to Bargara, she had already begun to construct her defences. Con would only be living in his rented beach house another six months, then he'd be going back to Sydney, or Melbourne, or wherever he really lived. She could hang on that long, provided she kept their association to a bare minimum.

She was so engrossed in her thoughts that she didn't even notice when he took a different road, and the car began to climb up the side of the Hummock. But as they neared the crest, and her eyes began to roam across the miles of light-speckled darkness, she sat up straighter in her seat and exclaimed with excitement, 'Oh, isn't it absolutely glorious?'

She could see Bundaberg, and off to the left and much

further away a lesser glow that she assumed was Childers, while in the other direction were the various beach settlements and the almost invisible horizon line between the sky and sea.

Verna's excitement overwhelmed her; when Con stopped the car she bounced out of it and fairly ran around the top of the Hummock, stopping briefly to peer in every direction. Only when a gentle hand caught her own did she slow down and allow him to point out the various highlights of the three hundred and sixty degree view.

'It's too bad you missed the cane harvest,' Con murmured gently in her ear. 'From up here, it looks as if the whole world's on fire; you could almost believe then that this was once a volcano.'

She didn't reply, content to simply stand there, her hand in his and a feeling of exquisite peace pouring through her.

Then he spoke her name, very very softly, and as she turned towards him, his head blotted out the stars as he bent to kiss her. The stars came on again, this time in her own head as his lips roamed across her mouth, gentle as a whisper. He lifted his head only long enough to whisper, 'Verna,' again, and then his mouth returned and her arms crept up around his neck as the touch of them surged a tide of emotion through her. His arms closed around her, fingers splayed against the small of her back as he pulled her closer, and Verna's own body strained as she rose on tiptoe to draw him even closer.

She could feel his hands moving, caressing her with a gentleness she would never have believed, exploring her body and sending sparks of fire through nerves she'd never realised existed.

When he turned her slightly so that his lips could slide across her cheek, down the column of her neck to cross the straps of the dress, burning a trail into the cleft of her bosom, she swayed with his direction, her own hands busy on errands of their own in his hair, across the rugged muscles of his shoulders and back.

When his fingers followed his lips, cupping her breast and dipping expertly to release it from the suddenly-loosened top of the dress, she felt her breasts responding to the play of his fingers, and when he suddenly turned her and sought her mouth again with his own, she felt his own desire rising against her.

Never had a man so thoroughly roused her, not even close, she realised. And where others had automatically raised a voice inside her to cry 'No!', Con's touch had that same voice crying 'Yes! Oh, Yes!' The urgency of her response frightened her, because she couldn't, wouldn't even attempt to control it. If he wanted her here, now, sprawling in the grass at their feet, it could be no less than her own wanting, and suddenly she realised that not only was her heart singing yes, but her voice was crying it as as well.

Con's lips were burning against the soft skin of her breasts, and her fingers against his neck were urging him on while she cried, 'Yes, oh, please!' in his ear.

Her legs were like rubber, and she was unconsciously sagging towards the ground, pulling him with her, when the sudden brilliance of a car's headlights swam across her eyelids.

'Damn!' she heard Con mutter as he straightened and thrust her around so that his body protected her half-naked figure from the lights. Moving far more quickly than her own trembling fingers could have managed it, his hands swept up the top of her dress and fumbled the ties into some kind of union behind her neck. Then his arm was around her waist, almost dragging her towards the door of his car before he thrust her inside and strode quickly around to seat himself behind the wheel.

The engine roared and gravel spun out from the tires as he swung the car around and sent it hurtling into the twisting road down, driving with both hands clenched on the steering wheel and his eyes nailed to the beam of the headlights. In the ten minutes it took to reach her small house, he said nothing and indeed didn't so much as look at her, and although Verna wanted desperately to reach out, to touch him, she didn't. She turned towards him when the car stopped, but he was already opening his door and moving around to help her out.

Hand in hand they walked towards her door, and Verna's mind whirled with words unsaid, unsayable. She wanted to plead with him, you've taken me this far—don't stop. She wanted him to carry her into her house, into her own bed, where nothing could interrupt the fire that burned inside her, where she could give herself totally, completely and freely. But she knew, somehow, that he wasn't going to do it. The tension she could feel through his fingers in her own was a different one from what he had shown up on the Hummock.

If he says he's sorry, I'll kill him, she thought quite irrationally, but when they reached her door and he said exactly that, she looked him straight in the eye and demanded, 'Why?'

'It wasn't the time or the place for where we were heading,' he replied grimly.

He stood, looming above her, with both of her hands buried in his own. But their touch no longer held barely constrained passion, only a great tenderness that threatened to bring tears to her eyes.

'Will you come in?' she said aloud. And the voice inside her was crying, 'Please say yes! Please take me inside and love me, want me,' even as Con shook his head sadly. And she saw that he'd heard the inner voices as well, and something inside her rebelled at the fact that he could read her surrender, her need, and yet reject her.

'I'm not trying to trap you into marriage or anything, you know,' she cried angrily, unable to stop the tears that sprang from her eyes as passion turned to a blinding, fearful rage. 'Damn you—how can you *do* this?'

Her hurt bewilderment increased as she realised that her body was crying out to him even as she shouted out her anger and freed her hands to pummel them against his chest as frustration blinded her eyes and heightened her rage. How *dared* he reject her? Verna knew in her soul that Con had wanted her every bit as much as she had wanted him, and his quick return to self-control was nothing short of maddening.

She flailed out at him with her fists, unable to see him through the tears that flooded her vision. And then he was holding her, and her anger was spent in sobs that she couldn't hold back.

He stroked her, like somebody gentling a frightened animal or child, and her sobs magnified and grew until her entire body was racked with shuddering and then gradually the tide turned, and finally she stood, shivering against him, but no longer sobbing. She opened her eyes and saw the shoulder of his suit, soaked with her tears and stained by her mascara, and she knew her eyes would be blackened by it.

Con's hands lifted her purse from nerveless fingers, opened it to remove her key, and reached out past her to fit it into the door. And only then did Verna hear the frenzied whining and scratching as Sheba struggled to join them.

When the door opened, a black shadow plunged out to

dance in a frenzy around their feet, but Verna couldn't move from the cage of Con's arms. Her anger had gone, and so, miraculously, had her fiery passion. All that remained was a cold, expanding emptiness inside her, and she shivered, knowing that when he took his arms away the emptiness would swarm up and take over her world.

She knew her face would be a mess of smeared mascara and blotchy, swollen eyes, but she raised it to look up at him, afraid of what she'd see but knowing she must see it, no matter what the cost. But there was no laughter, no harshness, no mockery in his eyes. Only a great empty sadness that extended to his voice when he spoke.

'Anything I could say—right now—would be wrong,' he whispered. Then his lips descended to brush against hers, ever so gently, and he turned away.

Verna stood there, one hand raised to touch her swollen, trembling lips, and watched him leap the fence, step into his car, and drive quietly, slowly, away.

Then the emptiness she had feared did come, and she felt it close around her like a shroud, shutting out everything as she turned and went into the house, oblivious to the dog beside her, oblivious to everything.

She moved through the house like a sleepwalker, mechanically turning out the lights behind her, undressing when she reached the bedroom, and finally flinging herself down to lie rigid upon her narrow bed.

Sleep came not as a comfort, but as a dark, glowering curtain that flowed across her consciousness like a black river in which she couldn't swim.

She didn't dream, she didn't move. She just lay there until the heat of the rising sun and the whimpering of her dog brought her back to a semblance of reality. But the face in her mirror was that of a stranger, a stranger whose eyes were smudged, and whose features seemed strangely distorted. She expected to see shame for her wanton behaviour, but there was no shame. She expected to feel anger, but there was no anger.

Only a strange, wearying emptiness.

CHAPTER SIX

By the time she reached the office, Verna realised the wisdom of Con's actions, and she couldn't help but be thankful for his strength and wisdom. But what surprised her was her own reaction, once a massive breakfast and several cups of coffee had brought her back into the real world.

She had thought about it on the way into town, a drive in which she'd deliberately sidetracked via the crest of the Hummock and parked for several minutes while she considered her position. She wasn't angry, neither with Con nor herself. Nor did she feel the slightest shame in her reactions of the evening before. The entire thing had a vague, dreamlike quality, and yet she didn't think of it as a dream.

It had been, she realised, the closest she had ever come to the kind of ecstasy that dreams are made of, and she knew that she would never regret a single second of it. There had been a rightness about his kissing her, his caresses, and her own responses, and somehow that rightness carried over to cover the rest of the events as well. Con had indeed taken her so far, and no farther, but that was as it should be, somehow.

She was no longer the Verna of the day before; what he had called her obsession was gone. And best of all, she knew it didn't matter any more.

Her chastity was intact, but no longer a burden, no longer a subject of embarrassment or even of concern. It was a part of her that had somehow become as natural as her red-gold hair or the fingers that touched wonderingly at lips still swollen from Con's kisses.

As natural as the love she felt for a man who might never return that love, but who somehow, she knew, would never spurn it as valueless, either. She had, in a strange and in-estimable way, grown up. And despite the knowledge that she loved Con Bradley with every fibre of her being, he had somehow shifted from her fantasy figure on the beach at dawn to a much more complex, and yet strangely more simple role. He was her friend.

That knowledge brought with it a calmness that seemed to pervade the entire office, and Verna's heightened senses understood and accepted when Jennifer and young Dave absorbed some of the calm, and were unusually quiet throughout the morning.

When the telephone rang at eleven-thirty and a rumbling voice said, 'How about lunch?' the new Verna glanced at the work still remaining and said, 'I can't, honestly, but I'll cook you dinner if you'll wait until seven. We're a little bit behind today.'

'Red wine or white?' he replied with a soft chuckle, and Verna knew it would be all right.

'Whichever you prefer,' she said, 'and Con ... thank you for a lovely evening last night.'

'My pleasure,' he replied. 'See you about seven.'

Verna replaced the receiver with a sigh that brought a wide grin from Jennifer, and at the sight of it Verna quite calmly stared the younger girl down.

'Off to lunch, the both of you,' she said in mock anger that fooled nobody. 'An hour without you lot and I might manage to get some work done!'

She did, too. Enough work that she was able to walk out of the office right at five o'clock, knowing she had enough time to get home and changed while she put together a simple but adequate meal.

It wasn't until she looked out to see Con's car out front that Verna suddenly began to feel the butterflies come to life inside her. She felt panic for just an instant when he knocked at the door, but as she opened it to greet him, the panic disappeared as if by magic.

He was dressed casually, in shorts and a soft, short-sleeved shirt that set off his muscular shoulders and splendid tan. One hand held a bottle of wine, and the other carried a bouquet of flowers, which he handed over with an exaggerated flourish.

Verna took the flowers and leaned up to kiss him on the cheek as if it were the most natural thing in the world, while Sheba sprawled herself brazenly at his feet and whined for her share of the attention.

They ate a slow, leisurely dinner of chicken and salad, sipping at their wine and talking comfortably about various subjects of mutual interest. Verna wasn't surprised to find they had mutual acquaintances in journalism, even though she knew Con had been out of the business for nearly as long as she herself had been in it.

They talked about food, about wines, about the theatre and about writing. She admitted that she'd only ever read one of his books, and hadn't been impressed, and he grinned his acceptance before rising to survey the contents of her bookshelves. He spent several quiet minutes examining the titles, and Verna felt no hint of embarrassment that a large percentage of them were pure romances.

As he pondered the books, she made coffee and brought it back into the small lounge room, and after a moment he turned with a mischievous grin and slumped into an easy chair where he could look directly at her.

'I thought you didn't like my books,' he said with belaboured casualness, and Verna looked up with surprise.

'That's right,' she said. 'But ...'

'You only keep books that you like, don't you?' he interrupted, and she nodded her agreement wonderingly.

Then Con seemed to pause warily, and she could sense he was selecting his next words with great care.

'Well, seeing that I've somehow become involved in sharing secrets with you,' he said slowly, then paused as Verna pondered this apparent change of subject, 'would you like to share one of mine as well? At least that way we'd be even.'

'It isn't really necessary,' she said, and gained a slow grin in reply.

'Of course not. That's what makes it fun. But you'll have to promise to keep my secret as long as I keep yours.'

'You're trying to trick me somehow, aren't you?'

Con looked sorrowful and hurt. 'Would I do that?' he asked pensively, then smiled as she giggled in response.

'You really haven't guessed, have you?' he asked. 'I don't know whether I'm happy about that or not.'

Verna's confusion must have been evident on her face, because he laughed happily and said then, 'All right, I'll take you off the hook.' He rose easily to his feet and took her hand to lift her from her seat and direct her to the bookshelves.

'You read a lot of books by Con ... stance Bradley,' he said quietly, then broke into gales of laughter as she stood there, open-mouthed and staring at him.

'You? Oh, no!' she cried. 'I can't believe that! You're having me on.'

'I'm not,' he replied stoutly. 'But it's a secret, don't forget. Nobody knows but me and my publisher ... and now you.'

Verna looked down at the row of novels, novels she had

come to love for their tenderness, compassion, and the believable—or almost-believable—qualities of their characters. Then she looked up at the huge, pale-eyed writer of spicy thrillers. Impossible, was her first reaction, until she remembered the tragic sadness she'd caught in his eyes at the restaurant and later, in her own doorway.

'But ... but why?' she couldn't help asking.

'It's such a change from sin, sex and sadism,' he replied casually. 'I get bored easily.' Whereupon he returned to pick up his coffee and turn the conversation to other subjects, most of which Verna had trouble following because her mind kept returning to the improbable picture of the vividly masculine Con Bradley writing romances.

It was startling when she chanced to look up at the clock and see it was nearly midnight, and as if Con had followed her eyes, he expressed the view that it was time to call it a night. At the door, he took her gently by the shoulders and brushed his lips across her own in a single, tender gesture.

'Goodnight,' he said softly. 'It was a very nice dinner.'

'You're welcome; come any time,' said Verna almost shyly.

'I don't think too often,' he said. 'It wouldn't do for me to start getting too domesticated; that's something no bachelor should allow himself to get used to.'

The message was clear, and although Verna felt a tug at her heart-strings, she accepted it with a gracious calm that would have surprised the *old* Verna.

It wasn't until after he'd left that she looked sadly into her mirror, seeing not herself, but the two of them at the kitchen sink doing dishes. And she realised that for her, too, domesticity with Con Bradley in it would have to be something not to think about.

'Ah well, Sheba, I've always got you,' she said, leaning

down to scratch behind flopping ears that heard her words without understanding the pain and sweet sorrow behind them.

Young David took sick the next day, and the rush of handling both his work and her own kept Verna's thoughts concentrated quite fully on the office for the rest of that week. The weekend wasn't so easy to handle, but she coped by giving the house an unneeded cleaning and walking for miles along the beaches with Sheba.

But it was circumstance and not design that took her from the office at lunch-time on Monday, when she would have been waiting with considerable anticipation for Con's arrival with his column.

Reg Williamson created the circumstances, calling her into his office almost as soon as she walked into work that morning.

'I've just volunteered you,' he said, and Verna immediately grew tense at the implications. The publisher grinned at her suspicious reaction and waved towards one of the large chairs near his desk. 'Relax, Verna, what I've volunteered you for will be a piece of cake,' he said. 'Only one afternoon and one evening out of your young life, and it'll be a good public relations exercise for the paper.'

'One afternoon and one evening ... do I get overtime?' she queried, trying to hide her smile at his shocked reaction to that question. Con had been right, Reg Williamson was the original Scrooge, she thought.

'No, but you get a free lunch out of it today,' he finally answered. 'With my old friend Mrs Lansing-Thorpe, who is in charge of the annual Valentine's Day Ball.'

Verna could tell by his voice that Mrs Lansing-Thorpe must have been in charge of the ball for at least the last thirty years, but she sat quietly and waited for him to go on.

'You're going to be one of the judges,' he said—and

stopped. After a lengthy pause in which he carefully examined his fingernails in considerable detail, he handed her a slip of paper with an address on it. 'Mrs Lansing-Thorpe will explain it all to you,' he said.

Verna shook her head emphatically. 'Oh no! I want to know all about this before I go to lunch with Mrs Whatshername,' she replied staunchly. 'Don't forget that I've seen the kind of little schemes you come up with.'

'But this isn't a scheme,' Reg replied with a hurt look on his face. 'It's just as I've said; you're to be one of the judges of the Miss Valentine competition. They have the judging the afternoon of the day before the ball, and finalise it during an evening-wear competition at the ball itself. That's all there is to it.'

'Then why do you look so guilty?' Verna asked calmly, marvelling at herself for daring to be quite so strict in standing up to her publisher. In actual fact, Reg Williamson's cherubic countenance almost always looked guilty, but this time she felt there just might be a reason for it.

'I'm not looking guilty; I'm busy,' he said haughtily. 'Now off you go, Verna. You've plenty of your own work to do if you're going to be able to spare the time to lunch with Mrs Lansing-Thorpe.' The dismissal was clear enough, and Verna left the room with the note in her hand and a feeling of great apprehension in her mind.

Jennifer provided the clue. 'Oh, don't tell me they've got you roped into that,' she cried. 'You'll be sorry, Verna. Melba Lansing-Thorpe couldn't organise her own dinner. The Valentine's Day ball gets to be a worse fiasco every year it's held.'

It took very little prompting for Verna to learn that Mrs Lansing-Thorpe, one of the city's primary socialites, was a classic example of her breed. She was an impossible organiser, but each year somehow managed to co-opt enough people to arrange yet another Valentine's Day beauty pageant and ball. If it was a smashing success, which was rare, she took all the credit; if it flopped, the poor volunteers got all the flak.

'Actually, you might be able to cope with her, provided you're prepared to take a chance or two,' Jennifer mused. 'I mean, she's a real old blue-rinse dragon, but only because the locals allow her to get away with it. Somebody new, like you, might be able to shift her far enough out of the way to get the job done with no hassles at all.'

'Oh, sure. I can just see her running to Mr Williamson after I'd done it, too. It would be more than my job's worth,' said Verna. 'I don't even have to ask you to know he's scared silly of her. It was written all over his face.'

'Well, you could always pull your Dragon Lady the Editor act; she's just about dumb enough to fall for it,' said Jennifer with a broad grin. 'If she starts to get out of line, threaten to turn her into a cane toad.'

'That is not funny, Jennifer,' Verna replied, trying to stifle a grin of her own. 'But I just might try it anyway.'

Even her false bravado deserted Verna, however, when she knocked at the door of the sumptuous Lansing-Thorpe home and was greeted by a dour old man who could only be the butler. And a classic example, at that, she thought quite irreverently, stifling a giggle at the cadaverous appearance and stiff, over-correct manner. He looked as if a smile would crack his face and ruin him forever.

But at least he was some warning about what Verna might expect from the lady of the manor, and it was a good warning at that. Mrs Lansing-Thorpe was every inch the blue-rinse dragon Jennifer had described. Tall, thin to the point of outright scrawniness, and far from attractive, she looked like exactly what she was—a poor farmer's daughter who'd clawed her way into a position of money and power and wanted to be sure nobody ever forgot it. Small-town aristocracy at its ultimate worst, Verna decided on first impressions, wondering vaguely if the man who had brought this harridan into his own society had been blind, deaf or just desperate. Or in love, came an unbidden thought, making Verna instantly ashamed of her first impression.

But only for an instant. Then Mrs Lansing-Thorpe began to speak, and within three minutes Verna knew Reg Williamson had conned her again; Jennifer had been all too right.

She was searching desperately for the right words to form her refusal to become involved in this entire scheme, and knowing she might as well save her breath, when the sound of the doorbell interrupted her thoughts. Then the butler, impassive and correct as always, entered the sitting room to announce the arrival of Mr Conal Bradley, and Verna's heart gave a leap of alarm. Behind the butler, a tall, well-dressed figure moved into the room, nodding correctly to Verna but aiming straight for the lanky figure of Mrs Lansing-Thorpe.

Con looked every inch the authoritative, dominant figure she expected, and Verna wasn't overly surprised when he greeted their hostess with a continental kiss on the hand that quite obviously won the old lady's approval. A moment later they received drinks from the butler, and Mrs Lansing-Thorpe began again to outline the plans she had been making for the Valentine's Day Ball.

Verna only half paid attention, her eyes more on Con Bradley than on their hostess, and she wasn't surprised to see his expression mirroring her own feelings about the assumptions being made concerning their involvement.

When a ringing telephone somewhere else in the house brought the butler to request Mrs Lansing-Thorpe's attention, both Verna and Con almost sighed with relief. Then Con turned to her with a curious light in his blue eyes.

'I think you know more about this than I do,' he said grimly. 'Mind filling me in?'

With half an eye on the doorway, Verna quickly sketched in her own conversation with Reg Williamson, and then added Jennifer's comments on the issue.

'Right,' said Con with a wry grin. 'Time our old mate the publisher got a taste of his own medicine, I reckon.'

His expression told Verna enough to make her dubious, but he laughed harshly at her objections and fears of her own position.

'You just leave it to me,' he chuckled, devils dancing in his eyes. 'Leave it all to me, and if Reg gets stroppy about it, just say it's all my fault. I've got broad shoulders, so I'll cop the blame.'

Mrs Lansing-Thorpe returned before Verna could voice further argument, and from that moment on she was simply too astounded to argue.

They took their drinks and went in to lunch, a meal that Verna vowed she would never forget as long as she lived. Con Bradley changed before her very eyes into a man she didn't know, but almost believed in. He literally oozed charm and suave urbanity, all of it directed at Mrs Lansing-Thorpe. And their hostess absorbed it like a sponge, altering from blue-rinse dragon to simpering schoolgirl like a flower opening to the sun. Verna had never seen charm like it; she wouldn't have been at all surprised to see her hostess swoon from its effects.

It was like watching an old movie, and Verna barely touched her food as she watched, entranced and unnoticed while Con captivated their hostess, drew from her all the plans and expectations of the coming ball, and half her life story in the bargain.

By dessert he had the old lady eating out of his hand, and by coffee time she would have cheerfully, Verna thought, abandoned the ball entirely to make Con Bradley happy. But it wasn't to be that simple.

'My dear lady,' he said then, reaching out to take Mrs Lansing-Thorpe's scrawny paw in his own huge hand, 'I really must apologise for dear old Reggie.' Reggie! Verna had to smother a giggle in her napkin, hoping she'd been successful in disguising it as a cough.

'Obviously he's guilty of horribly misleading you,' Con continued, 'but I'm sure it wasn't at all intentional. He's simply forgotten that Miss Grant has quite tremendous responsibilities with her newspaper, and I, of course, have my publishers constantly breathing down my neck. Of course we're more than happy to serve as judges for this most important function, and we shall. Indeed I can even promise you the third judge you're so worried about, so there's no need to worry on that score. But as for any long-term organisational involvement, you must take my word that Reggie intends to take that on himself. And of course you must allow him to help you. Indeed you must insist upon it.'

He went on and on and on. And with every word, dear old Mrs Lansing-Thorpe grew increasingly amenable to having 'Reggie' established as the mainstay of her organisational committee. But it was that third judge that seemed to Verna to be the trump card in the game.

Madeline Cunningham was one of the country's top fashion models; even Verna, who cared little for high fashion except as it concerned her work, knew of the tall, dark-haired beauty whose name was continuously being linked with that of some Sydney or Melbourne social figure.

To have Madeline Cunningham on the judging panel for a beauty quest in Bundaberg would put the crowning touch

on the affair, and Mrs Lansing-Thorpe knew it as well as
anybody. To the charm of Con Bradley, it was a superb and
and useful tool, and one he intended to use for all it was
worth.

'Now you must ensure that Reggie doesn't go all shy
about this,' he cautioned his hostess. 'He's inclined to, you
know, and he'll try and shift it all back on to you if you let
him. So you must convince him that Miss Grant and I are
simply too involved in other things, and that we wouldn't
be nearly as suitable as Reggie himself. You may have to
become quite firm, and certainly don't let on that I've told
you just how interested Reggie is about your most worthy
endeavours.'

He began to wind things up then, and almost before
Verna realised what was happening they were outside together and walking towards their cars. To her great surprise, Con said nothing until he was gallantly handing her
into the vehicle, stopping to kiss her palm as he did so.

'Don't break up now; she'll be watching,' he muttered.
'I'll see you at your office in a few minutes.'

Verna waited nearly ten minutes before a curt knock at
her office door announced his arrival, and Con strode into
the room and swooped to lift her hand and kiss it before
she could protest. Jennifer looked on in amazement, but
Verna could only shake her head in wonderment as Con
greeted her in that horribly exaggerated playboy voice.
Then she felt her lip twitching and saw the gleam of
humour in his eyes, and seconds later they were both en-
gulfed in a tide of laughter.

'Oh ... Con ... you are ... you're ... unbelievable!' she
finally gasped. 'Absolutely unbelievable! I've never seen a
performance like that in my entire life. Poor old Mrs ...
Whatshername never had a chance. And Mr Williamson
... oh, Con, he's going to be so angry.'

'And so he should be, trying to suck us into a deal like that,' he retorted in his normal voice. 'Rotten so-and-so! And don't start feeling sorry for him, either, because he set us up deliberately, and he's just getting what he deserves.'

Con reached into his pocket and brought out the envelope with that week's column in it, depositing it on Verna's desk with a flourish.

'You can read it while I give Jennifer a kiss for being so helpful,' he said with a grin. 'If she hadn't warned you about that old battleaxe, we'd have been in too deep to ever get free.'

And to the immense surprise of both girls, he did exactly that, leaving Jennifer with a look of surprised pleasure that quickly became a blush as Verna raised her eyebrow sarcastically.

'Well, I was going to thank you as well,' said Verna 'but after that, I think you've been quite properly taken care of.' Then she looked back at Con with a speculative gleam in her eye. 'And don't I get any thanks for passing along the warning?'

'My very word!' he replied, 'but you'll have to wait until tomorrow night. What I have in mind doesn't involve an audience.'

It was Verna's turn to blush as Jennifer's laughter shrilled through the small office, but it was Con who turned to the young journalist with a mock-fierce scowl. 'And don't you be getting wrong ideas, young lady,' he said. 'We're going to visit the turtles, for your information; my intentions towards your boss here are totally platonic.'

Jennifer, fortunately, waited until Con had left the room before she looked at Verna and shook her head wisely. 'Platonic—who does he think he's kidding?' she mocked. 'A girl would have to be made out of stone to maintain a platonic relationship with that man!'

Verna privately agreed, but with her own heart stricken by Con's words, she wasn't much in the mood to discuss the matter further. It was becoming increasingly clear that Con Bradley was making sure that Verna got the message: 'Don't get involved; I won't.' It was far too late, although he couldn't know that, but even so, the implicit reminders were annoying.

As she drove home after work that evening, Verna had a momentary feeling that Con Bradley would have been much easier for her to handle if things had stayed as they were in the beginning, when her own anger and dislike for him had enabled her to keep her distance.

The following night, she fully expected, would be torture for her, walking the beach with a man she loved, a man who didn't want to love her even if he could, who didn't want involvement, and who should have been doing something to ensure that it didn't happen—not placing both of them in circumstances that aimed at everything but the non-involvement he seemed to want so badly.

She rose in the morning determined to ring him and refuse his invitation, but in the flurry of a deadline Tuesday she forgot, and when he rang to confirm their meeting time, her heart did the talking.

CHAPTER SEVEN

'You stay here and be a good girl, Sheba,' Con said to the excited, prancing dog, and Verna wondered how it could be that this tall man could exercise such tremendous influence on the fractious animal. The dog settled immediately, with only a small whine of discontent when Verna and Con closed the gate on her.

'No way we can take her with us tonight,' he said in explanation. 'The boffins that supervise the turtle rookery would have our scalps if we showed up with a dog during nesting season. And anyway, we've got to have some tucker first, and I'm not keen on leaving the little horror in the car; she'd probably eat my seat covers or something.'

The restaurant he'd chosen was the Bargara Dine-Inn, a small 'bring-your-own-grog' establishment tucked away on a side-street in the little beach community.

'The decor is no hell, but the food's really good,' he said after stopping at the local off-licence to pick up some wine for dinner. 'And what's more, they believe in loading the plates, which is what I'm in the mood for tonight.'

Loading the plates was a mild description, Verna found when the lady brought an enormous platter of veal scaloppini and laid it before her. Con's serving of piquant steak was even larger, but it disappeared as if by magic.

'Now that is what I call a man-sized meal,' he groaned, heaving himself away from the table after a similarly huge helping of dessert. 'Just what I needed in preparation for a long walk on the beach.'

113

They drove in silence the short distance to Mon Repos, and it wasn't until they were out on the broad white sands of the beach that Con began explaining to Verna the true significance of the turtle rookery.

'It's only really in the last few years that the place has begun to get the recognition it deserves,' he said. 'It's probably the only mainland beach in Australia where significant numbers of turtles come to lay their eggs, and certainly it's the only one that's so easily accessible to people. In a lot of ways, that's a bad thing, because even now there isn't enough organisation to give the poor turtles the protection they should have.'

He and Verna walked slowly along the beach, keeping to the soft sand above the water-line and watching for the characteristic marks of the huge turtles as they plodded up to reach the nesting areas.

'You realise that we might not see anything at all,' he said pensively, 'even though the time is about as right as you can get with a high night tide. Then on the other hand we might get really lucky; it's just about mid-point in the season, and we could actually see both a turtle going up to lay eggs and some fresh hatchlings.'

He reached out to capture her hand as Verna stumbled in the soft sand, and she felt a thrill of inner content when he chose to hang on to it as they continued their walk. Con explained that the beach had long been known as the rookery for loggerhead turtles, but only in recent years had it become famous as well because of the nesting green turtles and the little-studied flatback variety.

It was the discovery and study of the flatback turtles by local scientist Col Limpus that had really begun to bring out the ecological significance of Mon Repos, he said, giving the impetus for increased control and protection of the area.

'That's why we're not using our torch, by the way. The researchers have found that too much light and activity can upset the turtles.'

A little further along, they were stopped by one of the turtle research team, who casually but determinedly questioned them about their knowledge of the rules that had been established to ensure protection for the egg-laying reptiles.

Finally satisfied that they were at least reasonably safe to be left on their own, he suggested a specific area for their investigation and left them to wander off and check on the arrival of yet another couple. It wasn't until then that Verna realised how many people actually had joined them on the long stretch of beach.

Con took up her hand again along with their discussion as he related more about the turtles, which nested at Mon Repos from November to March each year.

'The actual nesting is usually from November to January or early February, but the hatching goes from January to March,' he said. 'Most of the nesting turtles will weigh two hundred to three hundred pounds. The loggerheads and greens will lay an average of one hundred and twenty eggs in a clutch, and the eggs are the size of ping-pong balls. The flatbacks lay about fifty eggs, and they're the size of billiard balls. The turtles will lay up to five clutches in a season, at roughly fortnightly intervals, and they don't lay every year.'

Verna was fascinated by the information this man seemed to be able to keep as if on a tape-recorder in his mind, but she was also supremely content just to listen to the rumbling sound of his voice as they strolled hand-in-hand along the beach. She wasn't even looking any more for the marks of moving turtles, and returned to full awareness with something of a start when Con halted abruptly and knelt to trace with his fingers along a metre-wide scuff mark through the soft sand.

'Ah!' he breathed. 'We're half in luck, anyway. Quiet now, we don't want to disturb her if she's not yet settled into her laying.'

Moving like two thieves, they skulked along after the turtle, following the easily-discernible track until they saw her huge shape amidst a flurry of sand.

They stopped then, well away from the ponderous shape of the turtle, standing in total silence as they watched her flippers brushing ever so slowly to excavate the body pit. Then she used her hind flippers to dig still deeper and create a pear-shaped egg chamber. During the half-hour Verna and Con stood watching, they were so entranced by the spectacle that they were hardly aware of other dark shapes moving up silently to also stand in observation.

'She's started laying now; I'll switch on my light and everybody keep reasonably well back,' came a voice Verna recognised as belonging to the researcher they'd met earlier. 'Please don't get too near her head, and try to keep quiet.'

In the light of the researcher's torch, they could see much more clearly as the enormous turtle continued placidly with her egg-laying, tears streaming down the huge reptilian face.

'Why ... she's crying,' Verna whispered, and was astounded that her voice carried so well.

'No, she's excreting excess salt that she gets from having to drink sea water,' said the researcher quietly. 'And while she's on the beach, it helps to keep her eyes clear of sand.'

Everyone stood silently then as the turtle completed her laying and then used her flippers to cover up the nest before turning to lurch in heavy slow-motion movements back towards the sea.

'How incredibly beautiful!' Verna whispered as the behemoth finally staggered into the waves and disappeared. 'How absolutely wonderful that was. Oh, thank you for bringing me, Con.'

'My pleasure,' he said. 'But let's not go back yet. If we wander further along maybe we'll get really lucky and see some hatchlings on their way down to the water.'

They wandered along the beach then in a companionable silence. Verna didn't know what Con might be thinking, but for herself she was content simply to be there with him, touching him. She could have wandered hand-in-hand like that for ever, and was actually disappointed when they eventually reached the small headland that framed the bay at Mon Repos. Still silent, they turned and began to retrace their steps, this time closer to the waterline where the now-retreating tide had created firmer footing.

The stars cast a gentle glow as small clouds scudded across the moon, and Verna felt herself wishing that Con would stop, take her into his arms, and kiss her. But he didn't, even though his huge hands were obviously aware whenever she flexed her fingers in his. When he finally did stop, it was because the turtle researcher had reappeared, to tell them in a quiet voice that a nest of hatchlings just ahead of them was exiting to the sea.

Moving quickly but carefully, they arrived in time to watch the final exodus of the tiny reptiles as they scurried across the sands in obeyance of their instincts. Most of them, Verna knew, were doomed to an early death as prey for carnivorous fish, and she squealed with delight when Con reached down to capture one small shadow and lift it up for closer inspection.

The tiny turtle was a miniature of the huge female they'd seen earlier, although the patterning on the new shell was more obvious. Verna reached out a tentative finger to stroke the tiny reptile, and felt a pang of remorse as Con stooped to release it once again on its journey.

'Off you go, young one,' he said softly. 'And see if you can last long enough to come back here to make new little turtles some night.' Then he took Verna's hand again and strode more quickly than before as they returned to the car park.

But as they reached the end of the beach, he seemed to change his mind about being in a hurry, and paused to sit on a huge old log and light a cigarette. Verna perched herself beside him, declining the offered smoke as she stared out to where a passing ship cast its network of ghostly lights on to the smooth, placid sea. The feeling of peace and contentment that washed over her made her slump with a happy sadness and utter a small, weary sigh.

'If you're going to go all clucky and broody on me, we're going home right now,' said Con with an abruptness that startled her slightly.

'What's the matter with being clucky?' she asked lightly. 'And if you don't like my reactions you shouldn't have brought me.'

'All right, I wasn't trying to start a fight,' he said. 'But when you get that maternal look in your eye, I keep thinking you should be off looking for a husband instead of hanging about with me.'

'That is a stupid thing to say,' Verna flared. 'And rude as well, since it was you who invited me. I was really enjoying this evening until you started on this line, and I wish you'd just drop it. You've made it quite clear that you're not looking for a wife, and not looking for any involvement. So O.K.—I get the message. Now if you value your freedom so damned much, then take me home and go off and enjoy it!'

She flounced herself to her feet and strode up the path

towards the car park, not knowing if he would follow and caring even less.

It was bad enough, she thought, to be hopelessly in love with the man, without him continuously throwing it in her face that she was wasting her time. But she fought back her tears and vowed that her feelings for Con Bradley were something he would never, ever know.

'I'm sorry I got all heavy with you,' rumbled a voice beside her as she reached the cars. 'I've had a lot on my mind lately, and it's made me a bit stroppy, that's all.'

Verna made no reply, but after he had helped her into the car and got in himself, Con presumed her acquiescence and began to speak again. 'Has Reg said anything yet about me setting him up for old Mrs Whatsit?' he asked.

'No,' Verna replied abruptly, not troubling to hide the annoyance she still felt. 'But he's given me some awfully strange looks in passing; I don't think he's pleased.'

They discussed the various aspects of the ball, which Verna suddenly realised was only a fortnight away, and then drove in relative silence as she let her thoughts wander to what she might wear on such an occasion. It wasn't until Con had halted in front of her house that Verna spoke about the one aspect of things she'd found unusual.

'What are Mr Williamson and ... that woman going to think when you don't produce Madeline Cunningham?' she asked abruptly. 'Or have you actually managed to arrange for a nationally famous model to visit Bundaberg just for this occasion?'

'Oh, she'll be here as one of the judges, no fear of that,' Con replied with deceptive calm. 'She should be arriving on February the tenth, and I'm hoping she'll stay with me considerably longer than the fourteenth.'

'Oh,' Verna said numbly, mentally kicking herself for being so stupid. She got out of the car after thanking Con for the evening, barely able to trust herself to suddenly trembling legs. It wasn't until he'd driven away and Sheba was gambolling around her feet in the yard that Verna's mind began to come to grips with what she'd heard.

How utterly silly she seemed, having assumed that Con was only spoofing old Mrs Lansing-Thorpe about the possibility of Madeline Cunningham being a judge for the ball. And how incredibly naïve not to realise that with such a woman on her way to Bundaberg, of course Con wouldn't favour getting involved with somebody like herself. Thinking of pictures she'd seen of Madeline Cunningham, Verna could easily imagine the tall, glamorous model as a partner for Con Bradley. And it was an imaginary picture that brought pangs to her heart.

But how despicable of him to merely use her as a stop-gap until a more suitable candidate arrived, she thought with sudden anger. Then the anger was displaced by the knowledge that he hadn't exactly been 'using' her, since he'd given her more than ample warning that nothing serious would evolve between them, fantasies or no.

Still, it hurt. Enough to disrupt her sleep and leave her smudgy-eyed and dispirited the next day. Also angry, both at herself and at Con. When he called to invite her on a drive during the coming weekend, she had no trouble refusing.

'Why not?' was Con's immediate response. 'It'll do you good to get out of town for a change, see something of the country.'

'I'm sorry; I'm going to be busy,' Verna replied, and the tremors of anger in her voice were directed not at Con, but at her own inner weakness. Because she really did want to go with him, despite her vow that he could find somebody else to fill his time until the real woman in his life arrived.

'You're angry with me,' he said with disarming accuracy. 'What have I done this time to get on your black list?'

'Nothing at all,' she replied lightly. 'And you're not on my black list. In fact I think it shows a great deal of conceit to even suggest it.'

'Oh,' he muttered. 'I must have done something even worse than usual. But not to worry; a quiet day's drive in the country will put you right. You'll have to be up early though; I've got a fair day's trekking planned. How's seven o'clock suit you?'

'Didn't you listen to me?' Verna snapped with renewed anger, and this time it was fairly directed at this infuriating voice that had so abruptly ignored her rejections. 'I am going to be busy, Con. I am *not* coming with you.'

'What have you got planned, then?'

It was so abrupt that Verna was caught offguard, a situation not at all improved by the fact she had nothing whatsoever planned, and suspected he knew it.

'It's absolutely none of your business what I've got planned,' she replied with as much dignity as she could muster. 'The point of the issue is that I cannot go with you on Saturday. Now if you've nothing else to discuss, I have a great deal of work to do.'

'My word, but you're shirty,' he chuckled. 'And I can't for the life of me imagine why. Ah well, you'll be over it by Saturday. See you ...' And he was gone, leaving Verna staring angrily at the silent telephone.

Her anger grew, rather than diminished, and when she finally tucked into bed on Friday night still without the slightest idea what she'd do the next day, except that it wouldn't involve Con Bradley—she was half tempted to go around and bang on his door and have it out right there, despite the lateness of the hour. She was still thinking about it when she finally drifted off to sleep, having set her alarm for six so that if nothing else she could be well away from the house just in case he did call for her at seven o'clock.

By six-thirty next morning she was awake, showered, dressed and waiting for the coffee to finish perking when a knock at the door made her leap to her feet in surprise. Before she could reach the door, however, it opened to admit a smiling Con Bradley.

'Coffee! Good ... just what I needed,' he said with a grin, strolling over to seat himself beside Verna's chair.

'What are you *doing* here?' Verna asked with astonishment evident in her eyes.

'Waiting for you to pour me some coffee. Or am I expected to pour my own?' Lounging back in his chair, he seemed totally unaware of how unwelcome he was. Verna stood up and moved to the counter, then stopped herself in amazement as she found herself reaching up for a second coffee mug.

What am I doing? she wondered. The absolute nerve of this ... this egotistical character, expecting me to just hop up and get his coffee! Turning, she stood and stared at the intruder, unable to help herself from noticing just how masculine he was in a short-sleeved shirt open to the waist and shorts that revealed his well-tanned, powerful legs.

'You just get out of here,' she said finally with a determined frown. 'I've already said I'm going to be busy today ... and I am! Now you know I'm not going anywhere with you, so please leave.'

'Without even a cup of coffee? That's not very neighbourly, I must say,' he answered without shifting his relaxed position.

'Oh, all right! Have your damned coffee and then go,' Verna replied hotly. 'But I honestly think you're taking an awful lot for granted.'

Con said nothing until he thanked her for the coffee,

which he drank slowly without taking his eyes from her.

She could feel herself tingling beneath his frankly disrupting appraisal, but she managed to keep her own silence, staring angrily out the window as she wished he'd finish his coffee and get out.

'What are you planning today that's so terribly important?' he asked suddenly.

'I keep telling you ... it's none of your business,' she shot back.

'But how can I persuade you to change your mind if you won't tell me what your plans are?' he replied gently.

'Oh, all right,' she replied hastily. 'I'm ...'

'... lying to me; that's what you're doing,' he said. 'You know very well you haven't any plans at all. What I can't understand is why you insist on trying to lie to me, Verna. You should know by now that I can read your mind.'

'I am not lying,' she lied. 'I'm spending the day in the office getting my story bank up to scratch. With Dave sick we had to use up a lot of features, and I'm afraid the stockpile's got too low for my satisfaction.'

She turned to look Con directly in the eye as she dreamed up and spoke the blatant lie, so she couldn't miss the mocking laughter that sprang up, seeming to flare even brighter with her every word.

'Bulldust!' he said when she'd finished. 'You're the worst liar in the entire world, my girl, which is likely just as well if *that's* the best excuse you can manage.'

He rose and strolled over to pour himself more coffee while Verna, who had felt a surge of relief that he was leaving after all, sat in stunned silence as he mixed in the milk and sugar and returned to his seat.

'Look, if you honestly don't want to come with me, why not just say so?' he asked. 'I mean, I'm not a schoolboy; I'm not going to break down and cry or anything. At least it would be better than all this prevaricating.'

'All right. I don't want to go with you today. I don't want to go with you tomorrow. I didn't want you here. I don't like you bursting in here expecting to be fed and watered. And I want you gone! Is that clear enough, Mr Bradley? Gone!' Verna was near to tears by the time she'd finished, and only just managed to choke out a final, 'Is that good enough for you?'

Con was unmoved. He lounged back in his chair and shot her a quizzical glance from those bright, pale blue eyes. 'Why are you so mad at me?' he asked softly. 'And don't tell me it's none of my business. You were fine the last time I saw you, if not exactly loving, and now you've gone all hostile and out-of-my-life-you-cad. What the hell's the matter?'

'Maybe I just don't like being a stand-in,' she muttered, not quite realising how loudly the words emerged.

'Stand-in? For what, may I ask?' Con replied with a look of total confusion. 'What *are* you on about, anyway?'

But Verna, shocked by her own indiscretion, wasn't about to compound the error by repeating herself, much less by explaining her feelings to Con Bradley. It was bad enough, she thought, that he had only to look at her to bring her pulse to a fever-pitch, without having him blatantly aware that she loved him. She shook her head stubbornly, not trusting herself to speak.

Con sat with one eyebrow raised as he studied her face, deliberately opening his countenance so that Verna couldn't help but see it as comprehension dawned.

'You're jealous!' He shouted the accusation with an incredulous burst of laughter, his entire face lighting up with the amazement of it. Verna felt herself go scarlet, and turned her face away even as she replied hotly:

'I'm not! Don't be ridiculous!'

'The hell I won't. You are so. You ... are ... jealous,' he said quite deliberately. 'Verna? You mean you ... no, of course you don't ...' And his voice dropped away to a gentle, speculative rumble as he spoke almost to himself. '... and so you shouldn't.' Then his voice returned to normal as he leaped to his feet and stalked over to pour Verna a fresh cup of coffee. 'O.K., I believe you.'

She turned around in her own disbelief, so sure that he now knew everything, and so unsure of how he would react.

'You do? Well, thank you very much,' she retorted. 'And thank you for the coffee. Are you going now?'

'Soon as you're ready.'

'I've already told you I'm busy at work,' she said, but Con simply ignored her.

'I said I believed you about not being jealous,' he said, 'but this thing about working on Saturday is nonsense. You might as well come for a drive.'

'I am not coming anywhere with you, and I am not jealous!' she shouted angrily.

'So prove it; come along for the drive.' Con sat back in his chair with a grin quirking about his mouth as if he was laughing at Verna and not trying hard enough to hide it.

'I don't have to prove *anything* to you,' she said. 'Now will you please just take "no" for an answer and get out of here!'

'You *are* jealous,' he replied with a malicious gleam in his eyes.

'I'm not! I'm not, I'm not, I'm not!' she cried.

'Good,' he replied. 'So let's get going before we waste the whole damned day arguing. Sheba's already waiting, I see.'

From his angle he could see the car parked in front of the

house, and Verna rose quickly and walked around to where she could also see the dark shape of her dog lying patiently on the back seat of Con's car, which was parked with the back door wide open.

Flinging open the door, Verna charged out into the yard and rushed towards the car, shouting at the bewildered dog as she ran. 'Sheba, you rotten little black mongrel, you get out of that car right now before I give you a licking you'll never forget!' she raged, oblivious of Con moving right along with her.

'Sheba ... sit! Stay,' his voice rumbled, and the chocolate shape lifted immediately to alertness, sitting proudly on the rear seat with tail thumping against the other door and long pink tongue dangling in a broad smile.

Verna stopped her harangue and stamped her foot angrily, turning on Con Bradley with eyes flaring in their rage. 'How dare you? How dare you discipline *my* dog like that?' she cried. 'Oh ... what do you think you're doing?'

Con shrugged casually. 'Somebody's got to train the great gook,' he replied. 'It was supposed to be a surprise, actually, but you're a difficult person to plan surprises for. Why you couldn't have just agreed to come along today as I asked you, I honestly don't know ...'

'Do you mean you've actually been *training* Sheba?' Verna asked, eyes wide. 'What have you been ... oh ... what a colossal nerve!'

'Not really; just patience,' he replied. 'And being smarter than the dog, which helps a lot. Now why don't you go get your bag and stuff and we'll get on the road. When we stop for lunch I'll show you how smart your dog really is.'

'I thought I already told you ...'

'And I'm telling you that I've just about had enough,' he interrupted. 'I do not like having my surprises spoiled by tantrum-throwing females. Now get in the house and get your handbag; you're coming along today whether you want to or not.'

'I won't!'

'You will,' he said grimly. 'Now are you coming by yourself . . . or do I have to abduct you?'

'You wouldn't dare!'

'Oh,' he said, stepping over to reach a long arm down and clasp her about the wrist. 'If I have to, little girl, I'll tie you to the seat. Or better yet, I'll tie you to the back seat and let Sheba ride up front; at least *she* knows how to behave.'

Verna tried to free her wrist, but it was as if she were handcuffed to Con as he began moving towards the house, dragging her along with him despite her struggles.

'Sheba! Help!' she cried, feeling a surge of sheer satisfaction as the lean dark shape bounded from the car and raced over to them. But it was short-lived. Sheba thought it was a most delightful game, and bounded around them in a great circle, barking happily.

Con laughed at her antics, flinging open the door to haul Verna bodily into the house before he released her. 'Right! Handbag, swimsuit and towel,' he said. 'We can get tucker some place along the way.'

It was obvious Verna was going whether she liked it or not, but she refused to show any degree of acceptance. 'I want to change, if we're going anywhere to eat,' she said angrily, turning to stride towards her bedroom.

'Well, don't be long,' was the reply, 'or I'll come in and get you.'

'You would!' she snarled over her shoulder before slamming the bedroom door in his face. It took her only a minute to strip down, put on her bikini, and cover it with shorts and a bright, colourful tank-top, but when she'd finished, she deliberately sat down on the bed and played for time.

'Hurry up, damn it,' came the rumbling voice from outside the door, and she started guiltily before replying.

'I'll only be a minute more,' she shouted, and as she rose to her feet, the germ of an idea started in her mind. I'll fix you, you egotistical animal, she thought, tiptoeing over to slide open the bedroom window. Peering out, she could just distinguish the rear half of Con's car, with Sheba once again lying on the back seat.

Without a second thought, Verna grabbed up her handbag and stepped through on to the verandah, moving as quietly as she could until she reached the softness of the grass below it. Then she sprinted for the car, leaping the fence in a splendid bound before slamming the rear door of the car and flinging herself into the driver's seat.

She was reaching for the keys when Con's tall figure emerged from the house, and Verna thrilled with her success as the engine caught first try. This would fix him, she thought, already planning how she would drive off just slowly enough that he'd have to run to keep up, and once they were far enough from the house she'd speed away in time to return and lock herself inside before he could return.

'Sheba ... Guard!' The voice startled her nowhere near as much as the sudden growl from behind her as the huge shape of the dog reared upright in the rear-view mirror. At the sight of her *own* dog suddenly snarling with flashing, ivory fangs, Verna was so startled she slipped her foot from the clutch, and the car lurched forward several feet before bumping to a stalled halt.

Con was already yanking open the door and reaching for her by the time Verna could even think of starting the car again, and in her panic she slid across into the passenger seat, intending to flee through that door. But again he caught her wrist, snapping a command to the snarling dog to make it subside on the seat again, then turning to Verna with chilling, icy eyes.

They stared at each other for a long moment, Verna with her lip trembling as she awaited his wrath, and Con with eyes that ever-so-slowly crinkled as laughter rumbled up from his massive chest.

The tears began before Verna could even think of controlling them, great, huge droplets that trickled slowly down her cheeks. She blinked away the first, and the second, but then the floodgates opened and she felt her face suddenly convulse. Then Con had dropped her wrist and pulled her over to snuggle in his arms as she wept and howled out her fear and her frustrations.

When it was finally ended, the shoulder and chest of his shirt was sopping, and Verna's eyes were bleary and swollen with her weeping. As she began to struggle to free herself, Con took her gently by the shoulders and held her away. She could see that almost-forgotten look of compassion and tenderness in his eyes as he spoke.

'My very word; you *were* scared, weren't you?' he said softly. 'I'm sorry about that, old love. I should have realised. But your old Sheba wouldn't have bitten *you* or anything, you know? In fact I imagine she was as confused as you were.'

He held on to Verna's shoulders until she'd fully regained her equilibrium, then released her entirely. 'Tell me— all joking and everything aside—do you really have anything else planned today?' he asked solemnly.

Verna shook her head, unable to meet his eyes.

'Right! Then you will come with me on that drive,' he he said. 'We'll give old Sheba a fine run and then you can see for yourself how well trained she's become. But only if you really want to. I won't force you.'

'I'll ... I'll have to lock up the house first,' she said tentatively.

'No, you sit here and make friends with your dog again; I'll lock up for you,' he grinned. And two minutes later he was back in the driver's seat and they were away.

Verna sat in silence for the early part of the journey, unsure whether she was still angry or not. But once they had cleared the congested streets of Bundaberg and were out on the open highway, she felt herself slipping into the enjoyment of the whole thing. Con took a roundabout route, obviously aiming more for scenery than any particular destination.

They drove out on the Childers road, then cut across the wide Burnett River at The Cedars bridge and up to the Gin Gin highway. Then he turned off on to a series of narrow gravel tracks that eventually brought them back to the bitumen near Wallaville. After they'd passed Morganville, heading almost due south, the bitumen ran out into gravel as the country grew steeper and they left the coastal plain and drove into the Goodnight Scrub.

Con drove expertly but quietly, only speaking to point out things of interest like the redheaded scrub turkey that fled its roadway dust-bath at their approach, and the various lizards they startled from the little-used track.

They stopped for a brief swim at Mingo Crossing, high on the upper Burnett where the water was glass clear and tumbling beneath an old, abandoned bridge beside the new one created of steel and concrete. Sheba swam with them, causing Verna great distress when the dog tried to use her as an island.

With seventy-five pounds of soaking wet dog scrabbling to climb on top of her, Verna wound up with several superficial scratches on her legs and shoulders before Con disciplined the surprised dog.

'Lord love us, woman,' he shouted at her later. 'You're going to have to take a firmer hand with that animal or she'll cause you problems later. Now let's go dry off in the sun and I'll show you how the training's gone so far.'

Verna lay propped on a blanket, astounded as Con put Sheba through her exercises. Sit, Lie Down, Stay; then a series of retrieves and finally the command to Guard. 'You'd better handle her with this one,' he said with a grin. 'I wouldn't want to frighten you any more—and besides, it's you she's supposed to be guarding.'

He pretended great terror when Verna set the dog on guard as Con playfully tried to grab her handbag, but Verna wasn't totally convinced.

'I don't think she'd really bite you at all,' she said. 'You're just playing a game with me, aren't you?'

'No way! Although you're half right; I doubt if she'd bite me any more than she would you. But that isn't the point.'

He paused to glance down at the growling dog that crouched poised before the handbag. 'Are you going to keep her like that for ever?'

Verna shrugged. 'Why don't you call her off?' she said with a grin. 'I'm just wondering if you've taught her anything more dangerous than guarding. What would she do, for instance, if I set her on you? Would she take your leg off as I've asked her to do in the past, or just rush up and slobber all over you?'

Con laughed. 'It's better that you should call her off,' he said. And once Verna had done so, he said very seriously, 'I haven't tried to teach her anything more aggressive than guarding—and I won't. You don't want a dog that's liable to cause problems by taking a chunk out of somebody on command. Sheba is big enough and she can look mean enough when she wants to that she could scare off anybody but the most determined attacker. And I think if anybody was really trying to hurt you, she'd have them quick enough without any kind of training.'

'Oh yes, I noticed that when you were dragging me up the front footpath,' Verna replied with a wry smile.

'Be serious, Verna,' he replied. 'When she's full grown and mature, she'll be a first-class watchdog, but you don't want her too aggressive.' Then he grinned disarmingly. 'And as for the incident this morning, you know very well I'd *never* hurt you; and she knows it too.'

If you'd never hurt me, why is it that my heart keeps threatening to break? Or doesn't that count? Verna's thoughts rose unbidden, but she didn't speak them aloud. Instead, she focussed her attention on the lean, tanned figure beside her, unable to resist caressing him with her eyes. It wasn't until his fingers reached out to claim her wrist that she looked up to meet his eyes again.

'You do know that I'd never hurt you ... don't you, Verna?' he whispered, exerting just enough pressure with his hand to bring her close enough to kiss.

'Well then, stop mauling me,' she retorted, jerking her hand away and scampering to her feet, only to find him upright and standing in front of her.

'That was hardly mauling,' he said coldly. 'But I take your point, although I'd really thought we were past the point where you'd get all virginal about a simple kiss.'

It was the wrong choice of words, and Verna could tell from Con's eyes that he realised it even as the words fell from his sensuous lips, but before he could even think of saying he was sorry, she turned and stalked away from him.

Surprisingly, he let her go, and she stumbled her way back up on to the roadway and across to where she could sit on the derelict bridge, staring blindly down at the rushing crystal water where tiny minnows flashed in the sunlight. She heard him shout at the dog to come and dry off, but neither of them came near her until Verna had decided of her own accord to return to the car.

By that time Verna's anger should have softened, but if anything she was even more angry than before. But the anger wasn't directed at Con, but at herself. She'd realised by the look on his face that he'd never meant his words to be hurtful, and even while she was staring at the water and apparently sulking, it was with the knowledge that her own sensitivity was more to blame than the man who had spoken so lightly of a turned-away kiss.

And as Con seated himself in the car, she could see that he was intensely upset by his words. His mouth was tightly drawn, and the muscles along his jaw trembled with held-in anger that Verna knew was directed inwardly, and not at herself. When he reached down to fasten his seat belt, she reached over to place her fingers on his hand, willing him to meet her eyes.

'I'm sorry I was so touchy,' she said quietly. 'I know you didn't mean anything hurtful.'

'And I'm sorry I was so damned thoughtless,' he growled. 'But honestly, I never even thought of it until it was ... too late.'

'Then forget it; I have already,' she said, lying a little bit, but suddenly finding it important. He hadn't meant to be hurtful, and Verna couldn't force herself into emotional manipulations about something that she knew had probably hurt Con more than it could affect her.

Impulsively, Verna leaned over to kiss him on the cheek, but she found the gesture halted when a great dark head was thrust between them, laving her face with its long pink tongue.

'Oh, Sheba!' she cried. 'Yes, I forgive you too. Yes, I do. Now get back in the back seat where you belong, you silly dog.'

As the dog moved back, Con grinned at her in acceptance of the gesture. 'It's the thought that counts,' he said gently, 'although whoever said that obviously didn't have quite that situation in mind. Now let's get a move on, or we won't make Mount Perry for lunch and I'll die of starvation.'

They were just in time to catch a counter lunch at the Mount Perry pub, where Con regaled her with tales of the old boom-town days in the former mining community. 'You'd never believe there was once a tent city of thousands here, would you?' he asked, eyes swivelling over the small remaining township of ageing buildings and run-down, almost abandoned appearance.

'How do you know so much?' she asked. 'Is there nowhere you haven't been?'

'Never been here before today,' he replied with a grin. 'But I've read all the tourist guides about everything within two hundred miles of Bundaberg, just to be sure I don't miss seeing anything interesting.'

Verna didn't try to stop the chuckle that rose in her throat. 'And having read them all, I suppose you then spend all your time seeing if they're right,' she said with a laugh.

'Yes, indeed,' he replied. 'Never know when I'm going to want a particular locale for a book or something. But if you think I'm strange ... I'd like to meet some of the people who write these brochures. They leave me for dead when it comes to fiction writing, and that's a fact.'

'Well, you can always find work as a dog trainer,' she replied. 'Speaking of which ... just how have you managed to train Sheba so well, anyhow?'

'Very easy. You're at work all day, so I've been picking

her up every morning and letting her spend most of the day with me. Terribly sneaky, and I admit it, but I wanted to surprise you.'

It was so boyishly brazen she couldn't help but laugh at the mental vision of Con sneaking into her yard each morning to sneak off with seventy-five pounds of willing chocolate-coloured trainee.

'It's the weirdest thing I've ever heard of,' she said, 'but it doesn't explain *why* you did it.'

Con shrugged. 'She's at the age for it. And if you're going to wander around beaches in the middle of the night, not to mention living alone, I just thought it might be nice if she was some kind of protection.'

'Against everybody but you,' she said pointedly, which drew only a laugh in reply.

'But you don't need protecting from me,' he finally said with a weary shake of his tobacco-coloured hair. 'And besides, you've always got your handy-dandy little carving knife.'

'That was a low blow,' Verna retorted. 'Although I'm not so awfully sure that I don't need protection from you, sometimes.'

The rest of the day sped past in a kaleidoscope of colours and impressions. They drove north to look at the huge Fred Haigh Reservoir, originally called Monduran Dam and still held to that title by locals who objected to the government's renaming of the scheme for a public servant, then took a windy bush track across to Yandaran junction before turning south again towards Bundaberg.

They stopped at the Avondale Tavern for a counter tea of roast country duck, and Con made Verna laugh throughout the meal by describing what he'd write about her for the next week's paper. 'Goodness ... if I was that awful they'd never let me in here again,' she giggled, only to be told: 'They will if you're with me—and you will be.'

By the time they finally headed home, Verna was weary from the long day's drive, but she forced herself to keep awake with the knowledge that Con must be equally tired. It had been, she decided, quite the nicest day off she'd enjoyed since coming to Bundaberg.

CHAPTER EIGHT

THE next day was far less pleasant. Verna woke with her throat on fire and sweat pooling throughout her bedding. It was all she could do to make herself a light breakfast, which was a total waste of energy because it only stayed with her for fifteen minutes and the effort of getting rid of it left her weaker than before.

Banishing Sheba to the yard, Verna took several aspirins and returned to her bed just in time for her nose to begin running like a leaky tap. She slept fitfully for an hour, then decided she'd best telephone Reg Williamson and warn him that she might not make it to work next day.

'I think he's over with Con Bradley,' the publisher's wife said when the phone was answered. 'Can I take a message or anything, dear?'

'No, I'll call him there myself,' Verna replied, 'but in case I miss him ...'

She related the problem to Mrs Williamson and then immediately dialled Con's number. He expressed no real surprise when she asked for her publisher, and somewhat to Verna's consternation he didn't even ask to speak to her again after she'd told Reg Williamson about her illness. Even after she'd returned to her bed, she found Con's lack of interest mildly annoying.

'At least he might have asked how I was feeling,' she muttered before falling asleep for the second time.

An hour later, she woke up screaming. She'd been alone, on a deserted beach, and it was dark. But not dark enough to hide the sleek black shape of a huge dog that threatened

her with ivory fangs and a growl from the pits of hell. Every
time the dog growled, she could hear a man's voice shouting at it, a voice that rumbled like the surf and yet seemed
to draw on some cord within her. The voice kept telling
the dog to get away, but the blazing eyes and slashing
teeth drew nearer and nearer ... and Verna couldn't move
quickly. She kept backing away from the menacing shadow,
until suddenly she couldn't back any further because of the
iron arms that were clasped about her shoulders. The
shadow dog came closer, closer, and Verna screamed.

'Dammit, Sheba, I'm not going to hurt her.' The voice
rumbled through her scream and the arms tightened even
more around her. 'There, there, my love. It's all right ...
it's all ... right. Just a dream ...' And the arms lost their
feeling of constriction as a gentle hand brushed the hair
from Verna's sweat-soaked brow.

Then the rumbling voice changed, taking on an air of
such horrible frustration and despair that it seemed to be
crying. 'Damn it, oh, damn it, you stupid animal ... I'm
not hurting her, for God's sake ... will you *please* let go of
my leg? Oh, hell!'

It was the sheer volume of that final outburst that
brought Verna entirely back to reality, and she fluttered
open her eyes in bewilderment to find them only inches
from a pair of pale, ice-blue, pain-filled orbs that winced
even as Con breathed a sigh of relief at her awakening.

'It's all right, love. You were dreaming, that's all,' he
whispered with astonishing gentleness. 'Just a ... dream,
which is more than I can say. Would you please speak to
this ignorant animal of yours?'

His arm helped Verna to sit upright enough to see over
the edge of the bed, and her eyes widened in disbelief at
the sight of Sheba, growling softly through the teeth that
were locked around Con's right leg.

'Sheba! You stop that!' Verna shouted, and the dog immediately released Con and sprang up to lave sopping kisses on her mistress. 'Oh, do get down, you stupid old thing,' she muttered, feeling herself weaken despite the support of Con's arms.

He laid her back against her pillow and reached gingerly down to lift his trouser leg and look with a grimace at the bright red toothmarks on his skin. 'Well, I guess I can't even qualify as a dog trainer, after that little exhibition,' he said with a rueful grin. 'Of all the times for her to get the message, why did she have to pick this one, I wonder?'

'Oh, Con. I'm sorry, really I am,' Verna said weakly. 'Are you hurt very badly?'

'Just my dignity, actually. She didn't even break the skin,' he muttered. 'Scared hell out of me, though.' He reached out to lay the back of his hand against Verna's forehead. 'You're burning up,' he said angrily. 'Can you manage to control this beast long enough for me to get you a doctor?'

'I don't need a doctor,' she replied. 'It's just a bit of wog, that's all ... honestly it is. If I could just manage some decent sleep I'm sure I'll be right by morning.'

'Well then, control her long enough for me to get your housecoat on,' he said. 'You're not staying here alone in this condition; I'll take you home with me, where I can keep a decent eye on you.'

'But I ...'

'But you nothing!' he retorted. 'I'll have no bloody arguments out of you and that's that. I'd just stay here with you, but I'm afraid your neighbours might get the wrong idea and Sheba might too. At least in my house she knows I'm the boss, so I'll be able to tend you without dragging her around like a set of leg irons.'

He was already lifting Verna from the bed when she

suddenly realised that she was totally naked, and her immediate reaction was to throw herself back under the soaked sheet with a cry of alarm.

It brought a low growl from Sheba and a snort of anger from Con. 'For goodness' sake, woman, I've seen naked women before,' he growled, 'but if it'll make you happy I'll close my eyes.' And after grabbing up her housecoat, he did exactly that, supporting Verna with one hand as he helped her into the garment with the other. 'Right! ... decent now?' he chuckled, and when she murmured her agreement he opened his eyes and shook his head sadly. 'Such modesty ill becomes you, my love, but now isn't the time to discuss it. You just sit here and tell me where all the things you'll need are, and you'll be back in a nice dry bed before you know it.'

Twenty minutes later, she was exactly as he'd said, and with only the vaguest recollection of Con lifting her and carrying her to his car, shouting angry orders at the dog while he did so. At his large beach house it was the same process in reverse, although Sheba was much less aggressive when faced by Con on his own ground.

There were no more nightmares as Verna slumbered her way through the afternoon and into the evening, waking only long enough to sip at the thin soup Con spooned up for her, and then to take more pills before dropping off to sleep again.

Her sleep that night was vaguely punctuated by the clatter of a typewriter and the soothing, pleasant sensation of strong, gentle fingers sponging away the fever from her face and body, but the whole thing was so very vague that she had only a fleeting remembrance when she awoke next morning with the fever broken.

Then she thrust away the covers and turned scarlet at the realisation she was once again naked beneath them. But before she could do more than cover herself again, the bedroom door swung open to admit Con, looking so ridiculous with an apron round his middle and a tray in his hands that Verna couldn't hold back a weak grin.

'Your breakfast, m'lady,' he said with an exaggerated flourish. 'Only tea and one perfectly poached egg in your weakened condition, but if m'lady can keep it down I'll try to do better for luncheon.'

M'lady did manage, but only just, and she was asleep again almost immediately afterwards, once assured that her work was being taken care of.

'It'll do old Reg good to step back into harness for a change,' Con had said brusquely. 'Maybe then he'll realise how much work you actually do with that paper, and he won't be so free at offering your services to all and sundry. So forget about work, love. Just go back to sleep and leave everything to me. If Reg can't handle it, I'll go in and do it myself, but not until you're feeling a bit closer to normal.'

The next time Verna woke she was still weak, but at least approaching something like normality. At least until she looked at the bedside clock to find it was nearing five o'clock. Her housecoat was hanging behind the bedroom door, and when she struggled weakly to her feet and retrieved it, she was overjoyed to find that there was a complete bathroom adjoining the bedroom.

'If you're going to have a shower it'll be short and without washing your hair,' came a voice behind her as she stood in the doorway, and the uncanny reading of her mind caused Verna to turn around more abruptly than she should have. She stumbled and would have fallen but for a strong arm that clasped itself around her waist.

'On second thoughts, no shower at all,' Con said with a shake of his head. 'But if you promise to stay rugged up you may come down and try to eat something. I don't imagine you'll be able to sleep again just yet.'

He kept his grip on her as they negotiated the staircase to the lower floor of the massive A-frame house, and even in her unsteady condition Verna couldn't restrain the cry of delight as she reached the top of the staircase and looked down.

The bedroom complex where she'd been sleeping led on to a balcony-cum-sitting room, tastefully furnished with heavy, comfortable chairs and reading lamps. The main wall and the balcony railing had been converted to bookcases and the high windows provided natural light.

The room below was decorated in cane, with the fabric patterns in cool blues and greens, but here again the bookcases were the focal point. The cane furniture extended into a large dining room with a massive table that must have been four feet by eight, and across the dining room was the doorway to the kitchen.

'It's absolutely gorgeous,' Verna said as they descended. 'I just can't imagine how anybody who owned it could even think of renting it out.'

'Well, it wasn't quite this nice when I rented it,' Con remarked drily, 'but now that I've bought it, I'll be able to eventually finish off with the effect I wanted.'

'Which means all the bookcases and everything is something you've done,' Verna said wonderingly.

'Well, I'm not just a pretty face, you know. I'm actually a fair carpenter when I put my mind to it.'

'Oh, I'm sorry ... I didn't mean to sound as if I didn't believe you could do it,' she said quickly. 'I just thought they were so ... you?'

'My very word—compliments, no less! I'll have to get you sick more often,' he laughed. 'Or is that too high a price to pay?'

'Far too high,' Verna replied, and then, suddenly feeling

quite unaccountably nervous, 'And thank you for . . . nursing me.' Her expression clearly revealed her embarrassment at the obvious knowledge he had gained in the process, and Con looked down at her with a quirk of merriment in his eyes.

'Come and sit down here,' he said gently, guiding her to the largest sofa and spreading a large, soft blanket around her. 'And don't be embarrassed, Verna. You have an exquisite body and you should be proud of it. Certainly Sheba is, judging from the way she guards you.'

He looked ruefully down at his leg, putting on an expression of such outrageously exaggerated pain that Verna couldn't resist smiling.

'Did she really bite you?' she asked. 'I'm sorry, but I have only the vaguest memories.'

'I'd show you the toothmarks, but I'm not exposing my irresistible legs to you in your weakened condition,' he replied. 'You might be tempted to ravish me or something, and I doubt if you could handle it fresh from the sickbed.'

'Well, I could always get Sheba to hold you for me,' Verna retorted, and then looked away in surprise at making such an audacious reply.

Con only laughed, then stooped down to kiss her gently on the forehead. 'Not on an empty stomach,' he said. 'Making love on an empty stomach makes your tummy rumble. So first I shall feed you, although be warned I'm not the world's greatest chef.'

He brought her a tall glass of lemonade, warning her off spirits for the time being, and retired to the kitchen with the dog at his heels, leaving Verna to sip at her drink and wonder at the cacophony of sounds from the kitchen she'd never yet seen.

It seemed only minutes later when Con returned to help her into the bright, modern kitchen and sat her at the table.

'I'll just put the dog out and we'll be right,' he said, and Sheba followed him obediently to the doorway. 'Now I want it understood—no digging, no stealing from the neighbours and no barking,' he said sternly before returning to the kitchen.

'And now, dear patient, do you reckon you can handle a little tucker?' Verna nodded uncertainly, not willing to admit that she was absolutely ravenous, then sat wide-eyed as Con opened the oven to bring out two scone tins.

'Oysters mornay,' he said, presenting them with a flourish as Verna marvelled at the ingenuity of using scone trays to cook them in. They dug in, and cleaned up the oysters with hardly a word spoken, then Con returned to the oven for a massive seafood casserole that smelled even more delicious.

'Take it easy with this,' he warned. 'If you eat too fast you might upset your system. Don't forget your poor old tummy's been empty for a couple of days.'

Verna forced herself to eat slowly by making a series of highly complimentary remarks about his cooking, until he finally bade her stop it. 'You'll give me a swelled head, and I do that well enough by myself,' he grinned. 'But I'm glad I could show you I have some redeeming qualities.'

'But I've never said you didn't,' she replied. And then, with a shy grin, 'In fact after this I think you'll undoubtedly make somebody a wonderful wife some day.'

'Too right!' he replied. 'I cook, I clean, I even do the laundry—which reminds me that I must go off and do just that. Nothing personal, love, but there isn't a dry, clean sheet left in the house and I won't have you getting back into damp ones.'

'Oh ...' Verna was as dismayed as she looked. 'But you can't ... but surely you can get some from my place. I mean ...'

'Sorry, we've been that route already,' he said with a

broad smile. 'Yours, mine and ours—all of them. Will you be all right for an hour or two while I nip out to the laundromat? I'll leave Sheba with you for company and there's a book or two I can recommend.'

He bullied over the rest of Verna's objections and returned her to the lounge room to be rewrapped in the blanket. 'I won't be long, and if I come back and find the dishes done or anything else, your bottom will be too sore for sleeping. I mean that, Verna,' he said stoutly.

Once she had promised faithfully to obey his commands, he departed with a basket piled high with soiled bed linen, promising to be as quick as he could.

Verna relaxed on the sofa with a Constance Bradley novel she'd never read, enjoying it with an entirely new insight now that she'd come to know the highly unlikely author.

Or do I know him, really? she wondered. Certainly Con Bradley the nurse and self-effacing chef was far more complex than the huge, faceless stranger of her fantasy morning on the beach. If, in fact, Con Bradley was that stranger in the first place. Verna was ninety-nine per cent certain he had been, but his deliberate off-putting of the subject left room for doubt.

Certainly she knew one thing: she loved him. And despite his stand-offish manner sometimes, she felt that just maybe he might be at least fond of her in return. But love, no! Despite the romantic novels he wrote and his occasional displays of genuine fondness, he was too reserved and cynical for Verna to give herself even the falsest of hopes. And besides, there was Madeline Cunningham, who obviously had the front running with the elusive Mr Bradley if anyone did.

It was think of the devil, with results Verna could have done without. Even as Madeline Cunningham's name

stalked unhappily into her mind, the telephone rang and
Verna answered it to the woman herself. She knew it even
before the caller identified herself, forcing Verna to do the
same with astonishing results.

'You're Dragon Lady!' the throaty voice on the phone
cried. 'And you don't sound at all horrid. Oh, I'm so looking forward to meeting you after all Con's said. You must
be braver than I am to let him write about you like that.'

Verna's astonishment at having been the subject of discussion between Con Bradley and his lady love made her
speechless for an instant, but if Madeline Cunningham
noticed she gave no sign.

'I'm just calling to say that I've had some studio booking
cancelled, so I'm coming early,' she said. 'I leave Sydney at
some absolutely ungodly hour of the morning, and I'll be
there on the first evening Ansett flight.'

Verna duly noted the times and promised to pass on the
message, expecting with every passing second to have
Madeline ask for an explanation of her presence. But there
was no such request, and when Madeline rang off Verna
returned to her book and her own thoughts, troubled ones
that seemed intensified by her experiences of the past few
days.

How would this stunning woman react when she found
out that her lover had been nursing another woman in his
bed? she wondered. Nursing, but still ... The intimacies
involved could not be ignored, and certainly not by Verna
herself. She had no secrets left from Con Bradley now—
except the knowledge that she loved him to the very soul of
her being, and that secret she must keep.

Con didn't make it any easier when he returned with the
fresh laundry and gratuitously allowed Verna to watch as
he remade the beds and cleaned up the supper dishes. He
accepted the news of Madeline's changed plans with no

more than a grunt, and said little until the work was done.

'I'm getting so well housebroken I can hardly believe it myself,' he grinned after pouring them fresh drinks and re-establishing Verna beneath her blanket on the sofa. 'Although I will admit I've been practising lately.'

He leaned back in the armchair he'd chosen and looked across at Verna with sudden seriousness. 'You joked that I'd make a wonderful wife, Verna, but, seriously—how do you reckon I'd be as a husband?'

Verna almost choked on her drink. So it was this serious, she thought with a jagged knife ripping at her heart. And obviously, that was why he'd bought the house, although somehow she couldn't visualise the sophisticated Madeline Cunningham settling down in Bundaberg. She tried her best to throttle the demons in her middle as she answered lightly.

'Oh, you'd make an even better husband. What wife could object to a man who cooks, cleans, does the laundry and even does home nursing on the side?'

It had been too light, she thought for an instant as his eyes narrowed speculatively.

'I did say seriously,' he repeated in flat tones that echoed the sudden chill of his glance. 'But if you want it this way, okay. How would *you* fancy me as a husband, Verna?'

She hid it beautifully, she thought, despite her recent illness. 'If I was looking for a husband, which I most emphatically am not,' she said sternly, 'I'd put you at the top of the list. Seriously.'

He raised one eyebrow for an instant, then lowered it with the acceptance of her words. 'And why aren't you looking for a husband?' he asked in the serious, friendly tones of a favourite uncle. 'You're not getting any younger.'

'I've got plenty of time,' Verna replied, her mind racing in neutral as she searched frantically and futilely for a way to change the subject. 'And besides, I'm very happy with my career.'

'So's Madeline, but I don't expect she'll be all that sorry to give it up for love,' he replied with a sober visage.

Oh, stop it, stop it, stop it! Her mind felt sluggish and she couldn't halt the jagged pains as her heart splintered into millions of fragments. She couldn't take much more of this without breaking down entirely, and she knew it only too well.

'Yes, but I'm not Madeline, obviously,' she replied. 'What I am is exhausted; if I don't get to bed soon I'm afraid I'll lose that lovely dinner you cooked.'

'Of course, I should have realised that,' Con replied with sudden tenderness. 'Come and I'll help you up the stairs. Are you sure there's nothing you'd like first ... a shower, maybe? So long as you don't get your hair wet it should be okay.'

Subject changed—and hopefully closed. Verna didn't feel half so tired all of a sudden. 'Yes, I think a shower might help a great deal,' she said graciously.

The shower was heavenly, once she'd laughingly rejected Con's offer to scrub her back. Verna lazed in the warm spray that seemed to strip away every vestige of her illness. The first wetting of her hair was accidental, but it was temptation enough; she quickly fumbled for the shampoo and gave her long tresses a thorough scrubbing.

'And if you don't like it, well, too bad,' she muttered, sticking her tongue out at an imaginary Con Bradley.

The reality was less easy to handle. When she returned to the bedroom swaddled in a clean nightie and fresh-washed housecoat, she barely made it into the bed before the bedroom door opened to admit her nurse and host bearing a tea-tray.

'Hell's bells!' he cried. 'I thought I told you to keep your hair dry. Oh, Verna, my love, what a damned nuisance you are sometimes! And to think I actually trusted you!'

Stepping into the still-steamy bathroom, he emerged a moment later with her hair brush in his hand. 'Right ... out of the bed,' he ordered, practically dragging her up to position her on the edge of the bed beside him.

'You may drink your tea while I do this, but you will not go back to bed until it's dry,' he muttered angrily, bringing in a fresh towel and scrubbing as much moisture from her long hair as he could manage.

What followed was so incredibly, unbelievably sensual that Verna knew she would remember it for ever. Con sat himself down and proceeded to brush her hair dry, pushing aside her objections with a brusqueness she could hardly credit.

His hands were so gentle, his every touch so hypnotic, and his entire presence so stirring to her own sensuality, that by the time he had finished Verna felt almost as if she'd known sexual fulfilment. His fingers touched at her neck, her flimsily-covered shoulders, at the lobes of her ears. His voice touched at her soul.

At first he chastised her for getting her hair wet, then he talked to her of his childhood, of watching his father brush his mother's long hair in this same way, and when she was almost asleep, her every nerve softened to a soul-destroying need for him, he countered by telling her jokes.

They were funny jokes, too, if slightly bawdy. But their humour couldn't compensate for her certain knowledge that he was doing it deliberately to stave off the effect he knew very well he was having on Verna's body and heart. Keep your distance, he was saying, regardless of the sheer cruelty he displayed by so intimate a gesture as the currying of her long, red-gold mane. When it was over, he didn't have to kiss her goodnight as he did, because they both knew he'd been kissing her with his hands for what seemed like forever as her hair dried beneath them.

Morning arrived with a shocking clarity. Verna was fully recovered, and woke to the scream of kookaburras with a clear head and a painfully wounded heart. It would have taken only one hint of encouragement the night before and she'd have given herself to Con Bradley with a deliberate wilfulness that surprised even herself, but he hadn't given her that hint, only the delicious torture of his voice and his gentle hands. Today she would leave.

That was what she thought until the whines of a plaintive and obviously upset Sheba brought her down the hall to Con's own bedroom, where the retching sounds from the adjoining bath told their own story.

'Oh, Con ... I'm so awfully sorry,' she cried as he lurched from the bathroom with his face pale as death and the sweat beading on his brow.

'Not your fault,' he gasped, then diverged on a long-winded explanation about where she could find the extra columns he'd written to keep ahead in just such an emergency.

'That doesn't matter right now,' she said angrily. 'You just get yourself back into that bed. I'll get you some pills; they helped me a little bit, I think.'

'I'll be all right,' he groaned. 'But you must stop Madeline; don't let her come here or she'll have it too. Get her into a hotel or something.'

'I'll take care of everything,' Verna said with growing exasperation. 'Now get yourself into that bed before I get angry. You've had your turn at being nurse—now it's mine —and I expect you to behave.'

'Not ... likely,' he muttered. 'And not as pretty a patient, either ...' His voice trailed off alarmingly, but Verna could see that he was only sleeping. She went to her own bathroom to get the pills, and when she looked into his for a glass of water, she judged he'd been in there most of the night with the early symptoms of the wog.

He came awake long enough to swallow the pills, then drifted away again, leaving Verna free to feed the dog and herself between checking on him.

By early afternoon, her worst fears were confirmed as he slid into a raging fever, and she spent most of the time bathing his sweat away. But she took time to telephone Reg Williamson and arrange for somebody to pick up the extra columns, and to inform him that she'd be staying off work, likely for the rest of the week.

Reg's objections gained him a savage reply that shocked both of them, but he accepted it willingly enough. That left Verna with only one call remaining, and she held it off until four o'clock. The clerk at the airport readily agreed to have Madeline Cunningham telephone Verna as soon as she arrived, and also to ensure that she didn't attempt to come to the house by herself.

Verna returned to her continuing battle to keep Con from flinging off the bedclothes and risking a chill on top of his fever. Her continuous sponging seemed to ease him somewhat, but as the sweat poured from his body she knew she'd soon be faced with trying to change the sheets underneath him. Rolling him over and accomplishing the tricky task turned out to be less difficult than she had imagined, and once he had stretched out to sprawl on his back against the fresh, clean linens, he seemed to settle just a bit.

It wasn't until then that Verna's own mind seemed to return to full capacity, and she was able to fully appreciate the beauty of the large naked body she was sponging at with trembling fingers. The dark hair curling at his chest flowed down across a muscular flat stomach to his groin before changing texture and colour on his suntanned legs.

Even in repose, the tremendous muscles of the man were impressive, and so, she realised, was his nakedness. Verna wasn't totally ignorant of male anatomy, but she'd never before been in a position to so closely examine any specimen, let alone one whose sheer physical beauty could so easily arouse her.

With a knowingly blatant deliberation, she examined Con's entire physique, memorising every detail of his face and body until he was etched into her memory like an engraving. A memory, for her old age, she thought.

So engrossed was she in her own daydreaming that she didn't realise, at first, that his ice-chip eyes had opened, and he was frankly watching Verna watching him.

'Am I beautiful enough for you?' he whispered in a strangely tremulous voice, and Verna's mind saw a very small boy seeking desperately for reassurance.

'Truly beautiful,' she whispered in return with a light kiss on his fevered brow. 'Now go back to sleep.'

Fortunately, he did, unaware of the tears that sprang to Verna's eyes as she looked at him. And even more luckily, the sound of the telephone didn't rouse him.

Madeline Cunningham took the news with a casualness that somewhat surprised Verna. 'I certainly don't want to catch whatever it is,' the model said with definite bluntness. 'And are you sure you should be playing nurse? What if you get it?'

'I've already had it,' Verna replied without really thinking 'That's where he got it from ... nursing me.'

'Oh,' came the rather flat response. 'Well, better you than me, darling. He's an absolute horror when he's sick. Half the time he wants to be mothered and the rest of it he's like a dog; he just wants to crawl off into a hole somewhere and be left alone.'

This particular confidence did nothing for Verna's own

peace of mind, but she was nonetheless glad when Madeline agreed to check by telephone each day until it was judged safe for her to come to the house.

The few times that Con was awake during the following two days proved to Verna exactly how well Madeline knew him. He was an absolute horror and worse, for some reason resenting his own weakness and taking it out on Verna until she finally lost her temper entirely and silenced him with blast of abuse that left both of them shaken.

Thereafter he was less fractious, but still so difficult to control that Verna knew a growing pity for every woman fool enough to consider being a nurse. Had she herself been even remotely this difficult? she wondered at one point, and then dismissed the possibility as being quite ridiculous. Nobody, in her experience, could possibly match Con Bradley for sheer, bad-tempered stubbornness and wilful disobedience. Literally minutes after he woke with the fever broken he wanted to be out of bed, and when she threatened to set the dog on him if necessary, he complied only on the agreement that she would read to him. It wouldn't have surprised her if he'd demanded that she read his own books, although luckily he didn't go that far. He chose instead some by the most romantic of his female contemporaries, and complicated the readings by interjections that were either embarrassingly personal or so cynically cutting that Verna could have throttled him.

And by the Saturday morning, there was absolutely no holding him down. When Verna, in desperation, threatened to hide his clothes, he said he'd roam the house naked, but he'd get up, and he did.

His first move was to telephone the motel where Madeline was staying, almost demanding her presence as quickly as she could arrange a taxi. This didn't impress Verna, who had planned to be away to her own home before Madeline arrived on the scene. Con's actions made that impossible, not least because of the immense pile of bed linen that required a lengthy stint at the laundromat.

But even more significant, in his eyes, was the need for food—man-sized food like steak. 'We don't have any,' she said, 'and besides, you shouldn't have such food yet. You need light, easily-digested food like eggs and things.'

'Hogwash,' he replied with what seemed to Verna to be genuine contempt. 'I'll starve to death on that kind of thing. Lord love us, I even gave you oysters, even if they didn't work, and now you offer me eggs. I want steak!'

'All right, I'll get some when I do the laundry,' she replied angrily. 'But I think you're wrong, and what's more I think you're still delirious. What's this nonsense about working oysters?'

She could have shot herself for walking into that trap. And for missing the gleam in his eye that expanded vividly as he told her the story of the man who ate a dozen oysters to improve his sex life, but only nine of them worked.

Whereupon he absolutely howled with laughter, not so much at the joke, but at Verna's expression when she realised he'd been having her on.

'It wasn't funny; it was typical male chauvinist piggery, which is all I'd expect from you,' she blazed in return. 'You are the most insufferable, arrogant, demanding, childish, boorish man I've ever met! I take back everything nice I've ever said about you. You wouldn't even be a fit husband for Dragon Lady the Editor. If she were real she'd turn you into a cane toad, and in my opinion that would be an improvement. I don't know what Madeline Cunningham has done to deserve you, Mr Bradley, but it must have been something absolutely awful, and the next time you're sick, well ... *she* can nurse you, and welcome to it!'

'Spare me that, for pity's sake,' he responded drily.

'Verna my love, you have no sense of humour sometimes. I honestly don't know why I love you like I do.'

'You don't, and you know you don't,' she flared, grabbing up the laundry basket and stampeding for the door.

Astonishingly, he was there before her, arms reaching to clasp her own even tighter around the basket as his whiskery chin nuzzled her neck.

'Dear Verna. It doesn't matter what I say to you, I'm always wrong,' he murmured as his lips caressed her ear lobe. 'But I do love you, especially when you're angry.'

Verna's anger melted with his touch, but she didn't dare to let him see that. 'You're just trying to butter me up so I won't forget the steak,' she replied, wishing he'd stop nibbling at her ear so distractingly. 'Now if you'll stop mauling me, I'll get out of here before Madeline arrives and catches you at it.'

To her immense relief, he did release her, and she flew out the door in her haste to try and outrun her emotions. It wasn't until she was halfway to the laundromat that the image of Madeline arriving to find Con in his under-shorts snuggling up to a laundry-laden Verna crossed her mind. Then she laughed, because it would have been so terribly funny and so terribly terrible.

She dreaded having to return to Con's house, knowing what she'd find on her return, but there was no way out of it, considering she had every sheet in the place with her, along with many of her clothes and some of Con's. She could only hope that Madeline had long since arrived, and that the expectable hugs and kisses were over and done with. Verna felt she simply couldn't bear to watch any soppy reunion scenes between the man she loved and the woman he had obviously chosen for his wife.

But she could, and did, bear it. Madeline's taxi arrived

almost in unison with Verna in Con's huge car, and
Verna was treated to the sight of Con—fortunately dressed
—rushing out to enfold the new arrival in his arms.

She sat like a statue, unwilling to watch the reunion em-
braces and unable not to, and when it was over she forced
herself to get out of the car and open the rear door to pick
up the high-piled laundry basket. Only she never got quite
that far before Con had turned and gripped her by the
wrist, literally dragging her to where Madeline Cunningham stood looking at them with the strangest look on her
lovely face.

Up close, she was even more beautiful than in her photo-
graphs, beautiful with that classic kind of loveliness that
can only be enhanced by maturity. Dark hair was coiled
stylishly above a veritable swan's neck to emphasize her
well-cast features. Her clothes, as might be expected, were
stylish in the extreme, and the body beneath them was
slender but incredibly feminine. But it was her eyes that
struck Verna most immediately, huge, pale blue eyes that
were almost exactly the colour of ... Con's eyes, and Verna
felt an immediate flash that their children would be similarly blessed. The thought shook her, but not so much as
Madeline's reaction.

Where Verna had expected a cool if not distant reception,
Madeline Cunningham rushed to throw her arms about
Verna's neck with a squeal of delight.

'Dragon Lady!' she cried, then pulled away to hold the
astonished Verna at arm's length. 'Oh, Con, you should be
shot! Imagine pinning a horrible reputation on somebody
as lovely as this! And you, Verna, should shoot him. I'll
even help you.'

She turned then and ordered Con to carry her luggage
into the house, since he'd obviously recovered completely
with such a beautiful nurse, and when Verna tried to pick

up the laundry, Madeline waved her aside and picked up the basket herself.

'You've already done far too much,' she said. 'And too soon, as well. Typical of Con to make himself sick just to get out of having to nurse you. He can be the most selfish man you've ever met—but I'm sure you already know that, after what you've been through.'

'If you're going to malign me you can just go back to your motel,' Con retorted. 'And you can go too, unless you've remembered my steak,' he glowered at Verna.

'Oh, get in the house before you make yourself sick again!' she replied with unexpected venom. 'I've had just about enough of you today already.'

'Yeah, Dragon Lady. One for you,' laughed Madeline, and Con, surprisingly, retreated with a chastened look on his face.

They were halfway up the footpath when Sheba came charging around the corner, and Verna shouted an involuntary warning as the dog headed directly for Madeline. She could visualise the reaction if Sheba did her usual thing of rearing up to plant muddy paws on that immaculate dress.

'You stay down and I'll see you in a minute,' Madeline commanded, and when the dog obeyed immediately, Verna wondered if she or Sheba was the most surprised.

Con had already deposited the suitcases when the girls reached the front door, and Madeline immediately handed him the laundry basket and knelt down to receive the ecstatic welcome of Sheba with an equally warm one of her own. 'Oh, I've heard about you, I have,' she said gaily. 'And you're even prettier than I imagined.'

All of which gained Madeline a friend for life, Verna thought, admitting at the same time that her own reaction was hardly what she'd expected. She'd been prepared for almost anything but the immediate flow of friendliness and

warmth that had passed like a spark between her and
Madeline. She couldn't help but like her, yet her feelings
somehow went deeper than that. There was an unspoken
bond that had existed with that first, unexpected embrace,
and Verna found it difficult to reconcile that with her feelings for Con Bradley, who would marry this woman despite
her own love for him.

'Oh, how absolutely lovely! How fantastically perfect for
a honeymoon,' came a glad cry from just inside the door,
and Verna realised that Madeline had finished greeting
Sheba and taken her first look at Con's house.

Verna began to tremble, and she had to fight back the
tears that sprang almost to the surface as she leaned against
the door jamb to counter the sudden weakness in her legs.
She simply couldn't face any more of this, she was thinking, when Madeline turned and dashed over to grab at her
shoulders.

'Oh, Verna,' she cried, and her voice was alive with
genuine compassion. 'You poor girl, you look as if you're
about to faint.'

She had her arms around Verna's shoulders by this time,
and was helping her towards the nearest sofa when Con
shouted from the kitchen, 'Who's going to cook my steak,
and when? I'm hungry enough to eat it raw.'

'Well, you can damned well eat it raw,' Madeline shot
back angrily. 'Con Bradley, you're a selfish animal! You just
come in here and look at this poor woman. She's absolutely
exhausted from looking after you, and all you can do is
think about your stomach!'

And then to Verna, 'You just sit here a minute while I
find the makings, and I'll mix you up a special drink. And
don't worry about the bottomless pit; he can just wait until
we're ready to feed him. Men are all the same. None of
them are worth the powder to blow them to hell, and much

as I love him dearly, that one will make the worst husband in the world.'

Con had returned to the room, and he too looked with obvious concern at Verna's pale face and dark-shadowed eyes. 'I'm sorry, love,' he said gently. 'I should have realised how weak you still are, but I thought ... oh, never mind. Can I get you anything?'

'Yes, you can get her a drink, and me too while you're at it,' Madeline interjected. 'And can I presume that at least here I'm no longer on show?'

At Con's nod, Madeline said, 'Thank goodness! Won't be a minute,' and streaked for the staircase as Con moved towards the kitchen to mix their drinks. Verna simply lay back against the arm of the sofa, wondering how she could possibly survive any more of having to share their happiness at the expense of her own.

Madeline was back before the drinks arrived, and Verna's eyes widened at the transformation. From high-fashion model to country waif in what seemed like seconds, she thought. Madeline had twisted her hair into a ponytail and discarded her fashion clothing for an ancient T-shirt emblazoned, 'Kissing a Smoker is Like Licking an Ashtray' and the oldest pair of still-useable jeans that Verna had ever seen. The change made Madeline look about sixteen, but it served only to enhance the sheer, vibrant human warmth of her. She was such an obviously genuine, loving person that Verna felt she couldn't help loving her even if she was to be the cause of Verna's own heartbreak.

And with the change of clothing came an unexpected air of authority. 'You are not to move,' she said to Verna. 'Or you either,' to Con as he entered with their drinks. 'I shall go and prepare massive quantities of steak and whatever else I can find. And when we're finished eating, you will *both* go to bed while I do the dishes. I've made up your beds already. And no arguments,' as both Verna and Con started to speak. 'Now where's my drink?'

The rest of the day passed in a blur of emotion mixed with alcohol for Verna. After two drinks and a huge meal of steak and chips, she still appeared ready for collapse, and was unable to argue when Madeline insisted on helping her upstairs to bed again.

'I just hope you don't have a relapse,' Madeline muttered along with a rather obscene comment about the quality of Verna's earlier nursing by Con. 'He should never have allowed you to get involved with that laundry, and it'll cost him dinner for both of us tomorrow night,' she vowed. Verna was too dopey to argue, and was asleep moments after Madeline left the room.

By morning Verna was fully recovered, especially after the lavish breakfast Madeline prepared. But when she so much as mentioned going home, she was shouted down by both of them.

'You're even worse than *he* is,' Verna said to Madeline in her surprise at the younger woman's autocratic manner.

'And you'd be a lot better off if you were tougher with him yourself,' was the cheeky reply. 'It's just like training a dog; you've got to let them know who's boss or you'll have nothing but trouble.'

The outrageousness of the statement forced Verna to glance across at Con, who was studiously ignoring their conversation. But he looked up at her with real surprise when she murmured, 'And here I thought all you needed was to be smarter than the dog.'

CHAPTER NINE

THE next few days passed in a blur of activity for Verna as she took up the reins of work again at work and tried to reconcile herself to losing Con for ever. Reg Williamson, unknowingly, helped a great deal. He'd made such a hash of things during her absence, totally depleting her stock of feature stories and fillers, that Verna had to work flat out just to get the paper on the street that week.

Wednesday morning, which should have been a relatively relaxed follow-up to the hectic Tuesday night's exercise of putting the paper to bed, was in fact even busier than Tuesday had been. And Verna's own inner turmoil didn't help. She was short and abrupt in her dealings with Dave and Jennifer, driving them just as unmercifully as she pushed herself.

She wasn't even fully recovered from her bout of sickness, she thought, or else it was her mental state that made her so constantly tired and irritable. She slept twelve and thirteen hours a night, but woke up tired and dispirited and feeling as if she'd never even been to bed.

The physical effects were so obvious that Madeline chastised her severely when the lovely young model walked into the office unexpectedly just before noon on Thursday.

'My God, Verna, you look like death warmed over!' she exclaimed. 'This won't do at all, my girl. The way you're going you'll be a zombie by Friday night, and we certainly can't have that.'

She literally dragged Verna out of the office, her take-

161

over attitude being more than sufficient to overcome any objections.

'We're going to have a delightful lunch, and then we're going to buy you a dress for Friday night, so bring your cheque-book. And don't argue with me, because I just won't have it,' she added. 'I've got enough trouble with Con; I don't want any hassles from you as well.'

But despite the pressure, Verna was able during lunch to avoid Madeline's insistent probing about her wan, unhealthy appearance. She couldn't possibly tell this woman, whom she had come to really like and admire, the reason for her condition. That she was dying inside because Madeline was about to marry the man Verna loved. So she lied, and for once did it effectively enough that Madeline accepted the excuse of a slave-driving publisher and a useless, frustrating advertising department.

But Verna had no such luck at diverting Madeline about the shopping expedition. Madeline dismissed Verna's initial objections and dragged her through every dress shop and boutique in the town. And her views on Verna's clothing sense were less than complimentary.

'Just because you're a working girl, it doesn't mean you have to dress like a prissy little old spinster librarian,' she said, rejecting out of hand a dress that Verna herself thought of as being rather daring and chic. 'It's a rag!' Madeline scoffed, caring not a whit if the the shop clerk heard her or not.

In the end, Verna was numb with the effort of following Madeline around, and when the younger woman's choice was finally made, she barely had the strength to tender an objection. Not that it would have mattered. 'If you don't take this I'm going to have it myself,' Madeline decreed, 'and it's absolutely perfect for you.'

The gown in question was a very simple design in soft,

clinging jersey of palest green. Slit to the thigh along one
side, it crossed her bosom to fasten over her left shoulder,
leaving most of her back bared and exposing enough cleav-
age, as Madeline put it, 'to spark interest in any man who
hasn't died without realising it.'

Actually it was no more daring than many of Verna's
halter-necks, but something about it gave an impression of
such sophistication and style that there was just no com-
parison. This was a really *sexy* dress.

'And so it should be, because on Friday night we're
going to stand this town on its ear,' Madeline laughed.
'Don't forget we've got all these spunky little Valentine
Queens to contend with—all of them young and nubile and
flaunting everything they've got. Competition's a wonderful
thing—after you've won!'

Easy enough for *you* to say, Verna thought to herself, and
then upbraided herself for being so uncharitable. It wasn't
Madeline's fault; Madeline had been first in the running
long before Verna had even appeared on the scene. And
she simply could not allow Madeline to realise just how
deeply involved Verna herself had become in the whole
affair.

But just once I'd like it to be me that's the winner, she
thought. Even if this time is the only one that will ever
really matter to me.

She managed to show a semblance of pleasure at Madeline's choice and her help, disregarding entirely the rather
exorbitant cost of the pale green dress. If I'm going to go
out, it might as well be in a blaze of glory, she mused, and
knew in her heart that with this dress, she wouldn't be
unnoticed at the ball.

It wasn't quite so easy at six o'clock on the Friday night,
as Verna put the finishing touches on her make-up and
swirled herself before the mirror. The sense of daring that

her new dress conveyed certainly didn't match her own mood, which was sliding closer to the bottomless pit of depression with each passing moment.

Madeline had rung during the day to establish that Con would be picking Verna up early and taking her back to his house, where all three could have a drink or two and discuss their strategy for the night's judging. And although Verna had wanted to refuse, the words didn't get out in time, and now she was stuck.

I'll just have to get through it somehow, she thought, shivering slightly at the thought of it all. She'd been psyching herself up all week for this evening, determined to somehow make it through the ball without breaking down and doing something either stupid or totally revealing.

Not too much to drink, eat as much as possible, and avoid Con Bradley like the plague. That's the ticket. But I can't be impolite, or start a fight or anything, she thought. It simply wouldn't be fair to spoil Madeline's grand night, not to mention her future . . . her future; Madeline's future with Con Bradley. Verna's own future had already been determined in her own mind. She could see herself as a forty-year-old spinster, probably as hard-bitten as some of the older female journalists she'd known in her career. Old and dried out and twisted and bitter, almost as dominantly masculine as their male counterparts. And while Verna knew she'd never sink quite so low, she knew also that she'd probably never know the happiness she so desperately wanted, the love, the sharing . . .

A soft knock at the door brought her to alert attention, and she drew a deep breath and steeled herself for the night ahead.

When her heart gave only a curious little lurch at the sight of Con Bradley, looking handsome as the finest of movie idols in his midnight blue tuxedo, Verna thought she just might survive. She hadn't broken into tears as he helped her into the car, nor even at the brightening of his eyes as he looked at her appreciatively.

The short drive to his large house was completed in silence, with Verna concentrating her attention out of her side window as she forced herself into a calm, almost serene acceptance of the evening ahead.

Madeline greeted them at the door with cold drinks already prepared, and Verna's first reaction after their hugs of greeting was that Madeline should be drinking something warm, not cold. The dark-haired model's dress was, as Verna would have expected, in the latest of fashion—the latest Sydney fashion, which made it almost shocking by Bundaberg standards. It wasn't a style Verna could have worn, and although she had seen one or two comparable garments during their Thursday tour, she had also been told by one sales clerk that not one had yet been sold because nobody had quite the nerve to wear such a garment in Bundaberg. And she could understand why.

But on Madeline it was breathtaking, because the years of modelling had given her such poise and assurance that Verna felt Madeline could have walked into tonight's ball in a towel and somehow got away with it.

There proved to be little discussion necessary about their role that night. Madeline dismissed Con's part in the affair with a casual gesture and a throaty, purring laugh. 'He's just there for convention's sake,' she said. 'He gets to peer at the young lovelies while we decide what's really important. It'll be just like this afternoon.'

Sipping at her tall drink of lemonade, Verna silently hoped it would be some improvement over the afternoon. Since Con had manipulated Reg Williamson into being involved in the ball, things had changed to put the informal judging the afternoon of the big event instead of the day before. It hadn't mattered all that much to the judges, but for the two dozen young girls involved in the quest, it had meant a hectic schedule of informal judging mixed with hair and beauty parlour appointments. Most of them would be arriving at the ball without a decent meal inside them, Verna thought, and she prayed—for their sakes—that nobody fainted or collapsed under the obvious strain.

And I just hope that I don't, either, she thought, staring down into her glass. But I won't! I simply mustn't.

She was dragged back into the conversation a moment later when Madeline suddenly put on a terribly serious look and leaned forward to place a hand on Verna's wrist.

'There is one thing that I must ask you, Verna,' she began slowly. 'Not about tonight, it's much more important than that. Now I realise that we haven't known each other very long, but I have found, and I think you have too, a sort of instant rapport. You've become sort of like the sister I've never had, and you're very dear to me ...'

Oh lord, Verna thought. Oh ... no! She's going to ask me something about the wedding. I know it. Oh please, Madeline ... stop! Please don't do this to me ...

'... and I've thought about this very seriously this past week, honestly I have,' Madeline continued, her voice and over-serious attitude forcing Verna's attention despite Verna's inner desire to get up and run, to run where she might never hear the rest of it.

'I want you to be my bridesmaid. Now I know it sounds awfully sudden and I realise you're surprised, but please, Verna, please consider it.'

Consider it! Consider the absolute, the ultimate blow to her entire being? Verna couldn't consider it. She couldn't even imagine thinking about it, yet she did. She saw a vision in her mind—herself standing there with a hollow, empty smile to match her hollow, empty soul. Smiling to everyone as Madeline married the only man Verna could ever love. She wanted to scream out her frustration, the pain that raged through her like an electric shock. She wanted to rise from her chair and flee, anywhere. Anywhere that she could get away from this entire situation, this blatant killing of her soul.

But she looked into Madeline's eyes and saw such longing, such honest wanting, that she simply couldn't free her own emotions. She too had felt the rapport, the closeness that Madeline had mentioned. And she couldn't hurt this other, innocent woman whose only crime was in loving Con as Verna did.

But even less could she fall in with Madeline's wishes, Verna realised. It would be nothing less than a form of suicide, for herself, and she'd never in a million years be able to carry it off successfully. She took a quick gulp of drink. Play for time . . . you must play for time, she thought, shutting her eyes as if in thought.

'Con, I think I need a decent drink after a real surprise like that,' her voice said. 'A brandy, I think . . . yes, a large brandy, please.'

Then she turned to meet Madeline's eyes again, and forced calmness into her voice. 'Madeline, are you sure you've thought this over enough?' she began. 'I mean, really, we hardly know each other and . . .'

Madeline waved a casual dismissal, her jewellery glinting in the suddenly harsh light. 'Of course I've thought it over. I don't really have many friends, Verna, not real friends. And I've never met any woman that I could take to as I have you. No, you're my choice and I'm sticking to it, provided you'll agree. And you will, won't you? Oh, Verna, you simply must!'

'But where is the wedding going to be?' Verna asked. 'I

mean, I have my work to consider and . . .' And I don't want to *know* where it's going to be, she thought. I don't want to know anything about it, except that it's over and I can start trying to forget . . .

'Well, we were thinking of Sydney, but I've changed my mind now that I've seen this house. It'll be here, of course,' said Madeline.

'Here? Oh . . .' Verna was stuck for words after that. Her mind whirled in a totally useless pattern of gabbling noise that refused to let her speak.

'Yes, definitely here. In the back garden, or maybe even down on the beach if it's nice enough weather. Oh, but that doesn't matter now. What matters is that you agree to be the bridesmaid. We'll sort out the details later; that's half the fun of it all.'

Fun? It would be agony. It would be impossible.

'Oh, but I'm not sure I'll even be here,' Verna said, desperately seeking an excuse, any excuse. 'I'm not going to be staying in Bundaberg, you see. I've already got several possible jobs lined up, and . . .'

'You can't possibly leave without three months' notice,' Con's rumbling voice interrupted. 'And this wedding is going to be held on the eighteenth of March, so there's no problem.'

'Now you stay out of this, Con,' Madeline warned. 'This has to be Verna's decision and I won't have you browbeating her; you do enough of that as it is.'

'The eighteenth of March,' Verna mused. 'Oh, but that's a Tuesday.' She breathed an inner sigh of relief. 'Oh, I'm so sorry, Madeline, but Tuesdays for me . . .'

'It's a Wednesday.' Con interrupted again, ignoring the warning look from Madeline.

'Verna, I don't quite understand you,' he continued, waving aside Madeline's half-voiced protest with a blunt

gesture of his huge hand. 'Now you know that you don't
have these job problems you mentioned. And even if you
did, you know I could wangle time off for you from Reggie.
And Wednesday's the easiest day in your week ...'

You know ... you know ... you know ... But you don't
know anything, Verna thought. How could you possibly
expect me to stand up with *your* bride at *your* wedding?
Knowing that it will kill me. How could you make love to
me up on the Hummock? How could you play with my
emotions and treat me like this? And how could I ever have
fallen in love with you?

She could feel the brandy burning in her stomach, lifting and rolling with real, scorching flames. Lifting, searing,
rolling ...

She didn't dare to speak as she lurched from her seat
and fled for the staircase, holding her skirts high as she
scampered up the stairs in a desperate bid to reach the
bathroom before ...

And she made it—barely. Through the sounds of her
own sickness she could hear voices from the lounge room,
voices raised in growing anger, one throaty and alive, the
other rumbling like thunder.

Then the door opened and Madeline knelt beside her, a
warm, moist washcloth in her fingers as she dabbed at
Verna's brow.

The spasms ceased and Verna moved to get up, but
Madeline's hand on her shoulder kept her there.

'Not yet, there may be more,' the other girl's voice was
soft, flowing with honest compassion. 'Oh, Verna, I'm so
sorry. I never meant to upset you.'

'It ... it wasn't you,' Verna gasped, feeling the shudders
gradually weaken and her body begin to relax.

'Well, I started it,' Madeline said. 'But maybe you're
right. It must be absolute hell to love a man like that. He's

my brother and I love him, but sometimes I could wring ...'

'Your *what*?' Verna couldn't believe her ears, and she felt the rest of the brandy flaring up again inside her.

'My brother. You know—the tall, dark, handsome *stupid* one downstairs ...' Madeline's voice broke off in sudden comprehension, then she fell silent as the rest of the brandy exploded like a bomb.

When that was over, Verna pushed away Madeline's hand and struggled up to seat herself on the edge of the bathtub, oblivious to any possible harm her dress might suffer.

The two girls looked at each other, a tremendous flow of knowledge passing between them like a silent, invisible river. Verna spoke first.

'And he knew,' she whispered, recalling his jests about her jealousy on the day they went for that drive. 'He *knew*!' she cried aloud.

Madeline looked even more shocked than Verna felt, if that were possible. Her ice-blue eyes flashed from cold to warm to flaming heat, and Verna shivered at the way they reminded her of Con's eyes.

'I was going to warn you that he's inclined to be a games player, a manipulative sort of devil,' Madeline said softly. 'But I guess you already know.'

'I do now.' Verna thought for a second she was going to be sick again, but the heaving changed to a cold, freezing lump of bleak nothingness that filled her stomach, her heart and her entire soul. 'I do now.'

She looked at Madeline and saw tears coming to match her own, and then both girls were in each other's arms, but it was Madeline's strength that provided the comfort, the stability, that finally ended Verna's weeping.

'Cunningham is my professional name, by the way, and

if it's any consolation, you've *really* got to him,' Madeline said then. 'Knowing him as I do—and believe me, I do!—I'd say he's fallen just as hard as you have, only he's fighting it much more effectively. But cruel, so damned, awfully cruel. I'm ashamed to be related to him, and I never thought I'd ever say that about Con. The stupid so-and-so has got himself so engrossed in the game he's forgotten the people.'

'I could kill him,' Verna said coldly, barely even listening to Madeline as her mind raced back to that horrible incident in her own kitchen. 'I could have, once—and God help me, I should have.'

It was as if they were each talking to somebody else, or to themselves.

'He's scared, that's it. My big, brave, bachelor brother is scared to death. He's fallen in love and he actually doesn't know how to handle it,' said Madeline with a sad, weary shake of her head.

'He knows I love him. He's known it all along,' said Verna. 'But he can't love me. How could he? Not and do things like this. Not so cruel, so selfishly, coldly cruel. It's because I'm a ... he said once I was too rare for him,' she faltered. Then anger flared again. 'I'll kill him ... I'll kill him ... I'll kill him!'

'You might have to stand in line, honey. Blood's thicker than water, and he's been manipulating me too,' said Madeline with a deadly softness. 'I think I'd like a little chat with my dear, soon-to-be-departed brother ...'

'Oh, no,' Verna broke in. 'No, please, Madeline.' She rose to her feet and stared into the mirror, seeing her blue-green eyes reflecting the emptiness that poured like ice water through her body. 'No, don't say anything. Nothing at all. It doesn't matter any more. Now that I know ...' she faltered only briefly, '... now that I know it was only a game, I can handle it. Honestly I can. And I don't want anything at all said, by either of us. It's over!'

Madeline's voice was soft and warmed by her compassion. 'You know better than that, or you will tomorrow ... or the next day,' she whispered. 'But we'll do it your way, only there are a few things I want to say first. So you start tidying up, O.K.? You can listen at the same time.'

Verna accepted the directive silently, staring at the stranger in the mirror as she did so.

'Con is thirty-seven years old,' Madeline began, 'which means he's pretty set in his ways. He's a hard man, a tough one, but he's always been a gentle and a fair man and I believe he still is, despite the evidence against it. And he's terribly proud, which is why I think he's gone so strange about this. He told you about his tear-jerker romances— oh, yes, he told me about that. In fact I've heard nothing but Verna this and Verna that since I got here, although I knew there was something up when he started sending me your paper every week. He's not exactly shy, but he's not the type to brag about things like his restaurant column, either. At least not to me.'

She made a parody of breast-beating, crying '*Mea culpa, mea culpa* ... damn it, I should have picked it all up quicker! But it's too late now and it doesn't matter. What I must say is this, Verna. When you two finally get it together, and you will, you *must* stand up to him better. He can't help being a manipulator; it's the way he was raised and he's too old to change.'

Madeline grinned wryly. 'Whole damned family's like that; I'm even worse than Con, but my man knows how to handle me. Oh, you'll love my Danny, I just know you will. Whenever I get out of hand he takes over and talks some sense into me, but I suppose Con's a bit tough for you to try that with ...'

Verna interjected, her own voice cold with the horrid,

vast emptiness inside her. 'Madeline, I know what you're trying to say,' she said quietly. 'But it doesn't matter, don't you see? It's over. Over, finished, kaput! I don't *care* any more. All I want to do is get this evening over with and forget it ever happened ... forget it all ever happened.'

'What a load of ... oh, all right. There's no sense in me badgering you as well,' said Madeline. 'O.K., it's over. You hate him and I hate him a little myself. But tonight we'll just keep our cool, and then we'll split.'

She stamped her foot angrily. 'But some day I'll get even with him—for both of us. You can't deny me that.'

Verna looked at her with empty eyes. 'Whatever you say, Madeline. Now let's get going before we're late. I just want to get this over with.'

'Are you sure you ought to even try?'

'I must,' Verna said flatly. 'It's part of my job.'

The two girls descended the staircase together, and Verna saw them through a new awareness. Her own beauty, for certainly it was such, was the perfect foil for Madeline's. While Madeline was tempetuous, wild and free, Verna knew that she was elemental, fire and ice, water and air.

And she saw in Con's eyes that he saw her beauty, and that it was affecting him. Then she ceased to notice. For her, he simply ceased to exist.

When he took her arm to help her into the car, and later, out of it at the Civic Centre, she neither flinched from his touch nor responded to it. He didn't exist.

During the judging of the pageant entrants, most of whom Madeline said walked like barnyard cows, she neither listened to Con nor spoke directly to him. She held herself in a reserve so complete, so all-encompassing, that he couldn't reach her if he'd tried.

She drank too much. Far too much, in fact, but it didn't affect her in any way except to fan the growing ember of cyclonic rage that whirled inside her, growing with every passing minute as her mind worked.

She thought of their first meeting, that lonely morning on the beach, and then rejected it. That wasn't Con Bradley. The stranger on the beach had been rough, but had given her compassion, tenderness, and caring. He had cherished her. Not Con.

She thought of her own responses to the real Con Bradley, the man who had almost made love to her on the Hummock, who had trained her dog, nursed her, and laughed at her. How could he? How could anyone be so deliberately cruel, so deliberately callous?

He had manipulated her from the beginning, treating her like one of his fictional characters. Without regard for her humanity, for the fact that she bled, she hurt, she cried. A game, that was all she'd been.

When the dancing began, Verna joined in with apparent enthusiasm, her eyes bright and sparkling and her body responding to the rhythm as it never had before in her life. But her mind was elsewhere, deep in a black, remote cavern where it stirred at a cauldron of bubbling hatred.

As the evening passed, she danced with Reg Williamson, laughing at his jokes and even twitting him about his relationship with old Mrs Lansing-Thorpe. She danced with one of the other organisers, and with several of the townsmen she had come to know. She did not dance with Con.

His first request met with a blunt refusal, and when it was seconded by his sister a moment later, he gave in to the demands from the winning Queen candidate and later her runners-up.

Verna danced, and drank, and danced some more. And the witch inside stirred at the cauldron as it bubbled hotter and hotter. Until finally she thought she would explode, and rose from her chair with the idea of seeking fresh air from one of the open fire exits.

She realised it was the wrong move when a large, tanned hand slipped around her wrist and she was literally dragged on to the dance floor, but she felt absolutely nothing as Con slipped his arm around her and stepped into the rhythm. Until he spoke.

'You're being very strange tonight, Verna,' he said. 'Don't you think you're taking this Dragon Lady role a bit too seriously? I'd almost think you don't love me any more.'

And the cauldron boiled over, spilling white-hot rage through her body as the tears spilled from her anguished eyes. Verna stopped dead in her tracks, eyes flaring as she lifted them to meet the ice-blue chips above her.

'Love! You wouldn't know the meaning of the word,' she spat. 'You're nothing but an arrogant, conceited, self-centred, manipulating swine!'

Con recoiled in surprise, then reached out for her.

'Don't you touch me!' she hissed. 'You've done enough already. You've taken me and treated me just like one of the silly women in your silly damned romantic trash novels. And I'm not!'

She stamped her foot angrily. 'Well, let me tell you something, Mr Con Bloody-minded Bradley. You're nothing! Do you hear me? Nothing! You play games, you manipulate people, you give them feelings and you cut them up and make them bleed, but you ... are ... nothing. Even your fictional heroes have more humanity than you, more compassion, more tenderness, more capacity for love. Oh, I pity you. I *pity* you.

'And I'd hate you, too, but you don't exist any more. Not for me. After this minute you are out of my life, out of my newspaper, out of everything I love and cherish and believe in. You ... do ... not ... exist.'

And Verna turned on her heel and walked away, leaving

him standing there in the middle of the dance floor, the other celebrants weaving a happy pattern around his rigid, unmoving figure.

Striding to her seat, she grabbed up her handbag and walked mechanically towards the front door, nodding her goodbyes to Reg Williamson and Mrs Lansing-Thorpe as she passed them.

Madeline, returning from the powder room, stopped her only long enough to whisper, 'I'll cover for you,' and Verna barely heard her. Walking tall and proud as any queen, she passed through the doorway and out into the darkened, quiet street.

She caught a taxi before she reached the corner, and she was home in her bed when the clock struck midnight.

CHAPTER TEN

SLEEP would be impossible, and Verna knew it even before she had stripped off her new dress and flung it in a heap on the bedroom floor. Even on the taxi ride home, the core of anger that had flared so brightly in the face of Con Bradley was beginning to flicker, to spin off some of its fury and solidity; by the time she had sprawled wide-eyed and wakeful for five minutes in her bed, the worst of the fury was dissipated.

Verna didn't bother to turn on any lights, she merely fumbled through the drawers of her wardrobe until her fingers encountered shorts and a T-shirt; then she shook down her hair from the crowning style of the night before and slung it back into a crude ponytail with a piece of string. She slipped into her thongs and left the house with Sheba an extra black shadow at her heels.

At first, she walked unthinkingly, revelling in the silence of the deserted beaches, the still, calm air of the sub-tropical night. She let her anger spread like a wraith about her, until it faded like night mist as the rising moon brought her shadow into stark relief against the whiteness of the sands.

She had come on to the sands at the north end of Kelly's Beach, and gradually her aimless wanderings brought her to the still waters of the lagoon, where generations of district children had learned to swim in safety, and where hundreds of sun-seekers would flock like galahs throughout the weekend.

By night it was another world, serene in its own peaceful

calm, with only the occasional flurry of a feeding fish to break the stillness.

Verna sprawled out in the coolness of the sand, her thoughts idly retracing her involvement with the man she now realised she would love no matter how badly he had hurt her. She looked back on her reactions when he'd first named her Dragon Lady the Editor, so recently and yet so long ago it seemed to be part of a past dimmed by time.

She remembered with an unexpected fondness how rattled she had been in that restaurant with Garry Fisher, and from there her mind leaped to the Chinese meal with Con, and her laborious trials with the chopsticks.

But it was over now, and she felt a certain sense of peace that it should be over. After her abuse at the ball he would never come to her; he was far too proud for that. And she was just as proud, in her own way. She would never go to him, she didn't think.

If only he hadn't been so afraid of love; if he could have given himself as willingly as she herself had done. If only . . .

Verna couldn't think about it any more. She looked at the still, gentle waters of the lagoon and wished she'd brought her swimsuit. Or that she had the nerve to throw off her clothing and let the warm, salty water wash away her sorrow and her pain, cleanse her. But she couldn't do that; even at this late hour the occasional vehicle passed along the road that formed the inland edge of the small lagoon.

There was one now, and to her indignation it wheeled into the parking bay on the north shore and disgorged a throng of young surfies, rending the night with their whoops of unthinking pleasure and the tinkle of their beer bottles.

No, thank you, thought Verna, splashing quickly across the narrow neck of the lagoon with Sheba at her heels. She was out of their sight in moments, and indeed she doubted if they would even have noticed. But their noise followed her, intruding into the lassitude of her thoughts, and she kept on walking south along the beach, well below the soft sand and as far as possible from the esplanade drive and the houses.

She crossed one rocky strip, then another, until her feet tired and she stopped on a tiny crescent of sand that seemed totally cut off from the world around it. The sound of the surfies was gone, the traffic noise didn't penetrate to where she was. It was delightfully silent.

Sheba went haring off into the shadows, but Verna hardly noticed. She stood, idly scratching at one bare calf with the toes of her other foot, and stared at the mesmerising action of the waves as they churned gently at the sandy beach.

She would go to Madeline's wedding, she decided suddenly. There was plenty of time for her to put her heart in order and muster the courage. Con would be there, of course, but not for her. She would make him vanish from her eyes as she made him vanish from her thoughts. It was easy enough.

She didn't have to think of his hands on her body, of his lips caressing her, burning fire that would never die in her soul. She could forget that, if she made herself do it.

She looked out to see a school of dolphins passing, their high fins cresting the waves like miniature sails. How wonderful to be a dolphin, to swim free in the ocean without the concerns and heartaches of love. Or did dolphins really have that freedom? They were almost as smart as humans, she recalled. Maybe even more intelligent, according to some scientists. Would that mean that they, too, knew love?

Suddenly she had the urge to join them, to know their exuberance, their swift freedoms. It took her only seconds to strip away her clothing and she was into the water and away, cleaving the waves with sure strokes of her own.

But the dolphins wouldn't wait; they disappeared into the moon's brightness, leaving her alone in the shimmering phosphorescence of the water. And even without them, it was lovely. The salty, tangy water laved across her nakedness like a caress, like *his* caresses, touching secret springs of tenderness and intimacy. Verna rolled into the waves, riding with the flow of them and diving beneath them in a joyous burst of pure, physical energy.

And when she surfaced, she heard Sheba's bark, a throaty, imperative command to her. The poor dog was worried about her, Verna realised, and suddenly was glad that somebody worried for her.

'Sheba!' she called. 'Sheba ... come!' And as she waved her arms, the black shadow gave one joyful yip and flung itself into the waves after her, paddling vigorously for the spot where Verna's slender, pale figure seemed to shine in the moonlight.

They played together for a time, until the dog tired and sought to use Verna as an island. It brought her memories of that drive, the beautiful, mountain water at Mingo Crossing. Too much ... too many memories, she thought. It would be impossible to negate them all. So, sadly, she turned and swam to the brightening crescent of beach.

Tears blinded her eyes as she hauled on her clothing, using the T-shirt as a towel and then pulling it on wet. It couldn't matter; it would wash.

Soon, too soon, she had reached the spot where Sheba had stolen the stranger's trousers. She halted, eyes involuntarily sweeping the sea and the sand, but both were empty.

Had it been Con that morning? It must have been, she thought at first, but on second thoughts wasn't so certain.

In her memory she could still hear the curses from the sea, and see the immense, masculine shape in the breaking waves. And on her lips, the taste of salty kisses that had fired her imagination and stolen her heart. It must have been Con; no two men could have such an impact on her physical senses.

Shaking her head, Verna raised her eyes to the emptiness of the sea, hoping against hope to see again that shadowy, fantasy lover, the one who'd kissed her but never hurt her, never torn her heart out by the roots and kicked it around like a football for his own amusement.

'I hope you drown,' she shouted with unexpected venom. 'I hope you drown and go to hell and I never see you again, Con Bradley!'

And the sea mocked her with its silence, laughing at her shouted lies as it tumbled the sand grains at her feet. Verna shook her head in anger and turned to stride resolutely away from the spot. She would never return, never as long as she lived. Twenty steps later, she halted to look back, and stood in startled silence as a tall, shadowy figure moved out into the moonlight.

It couldn't be! But she knew in her heart, in the very essence of her being, that it was. And although her instincts cried out for her to run—to him or away from him, she wasn't sure—she stood rooted like a mangrove, unable to move at all.

'Please.' It was the wind, she thought. The wind, or the muted rumbling of the surf. But the figure moved ever so slowly towards her, and she knew it hadn't been the wind or the sea, but *him*.

'Please, Verna. Please . . .'

Her mind shut out the voice. But her eyes couldn't shut away the approaching figure, only paces from her now, and she couldn't ignore the erect carriage, the broad, massive shoulders, the legs like tree-trunks beneath the ragged, cut-off jeans.

Another step ... another. She couldn't face it. She turned and sprinted like a deer up the shining beach, all her senses trained behind her to where the thud of heavier footsteps grew closer with every stride.

'Sheba! Sheba ... guard!' she cried, the sounds flying like seagulls along the beach. And out of the pool of shadows came a swift black shape with ivory fangs that flashed in the moonlight even as a bay of anger flowed across them.

The dog moved like death, silent except for that initial war cry, flowing past Verna in a blur of motion as it leaped for her pursuer.

'No ...!' The command turned to a frightened, angry cry of agony that wrenched into Verna's own heart like a dagger of ice.

'Sheba ... back ... get back ... oh, stop it, you stupid dog!' Even as she screamed herself, Verna was turning, eyes drawn with horror to where the mingled shapes of man and dog tumbled on the sand. And as the smaller shape disengaged itself from the larger, Verna flung herself down to take Con's head in her arms, oblivious to the tears that flowed like rain against his sand-strewn hair.

'Oh, Con ... I'm sorry. I'm so sorry,' she whimpered, then cried silently as enormous arms gathered about her to hold her as she sobbed out her frustrations and her anger and her love.

'It's all right ... all right ... all right ...' His voice crooned it like a song until Verna's body ceased to rack with her sobs and only shuddered with her fear now for his safety.

'Did she hurt you? Oh, please let me see. I must,' she

said, struggling to free herself from the living chains that held her against him.

'I love you, Verna,' he answered, the words tumbling from the heaving chest in a ragged gasp. 'I love you and I've always loved you and I'm so terribly sorry I hurt you. I'm a fool, a blind, stupid fool. But it was only because I loved you so much it scared me.'

'And I love you, you know that. I've loved you from the very beginning,' she whispered. His arms pulled her to where he could touch her lips with his own, and Verna sighed in ecstasy as their mouths met and merged and their bodies seemed to melt together.

Then she felt him wince, and felt his agony as it flowed between them like a brand. But when she tried to struggle free, he held her immobile. 'I love you. Will you forgive me, please, Verna?' he whispered, the words hoarse with pain.

Verna tried once more to break free, to get where she could look at his injuries, to help him, but still he held her, and pleading mingled with pain in his eyes.

'Forgive me,' he whispered.

'Of course I forgive you, you stupid, stupid man,' she snapped, startling both of them as the words lashed at him. 'But if you don't shut up and lie still and let me see how badly you're hurt, I'll ... I'll ...' She couldn't finish it, and anyway, his arms did move to release her.

Con's huge body flung itself back into a sprawl on the sand as Verna twisted around to run her fingers down the taut muscles of his legs. A cloud slithered across the dying moon like an omen, and she screamed out at him, 'Where did she bite you, Con? Tell me where!'

Then her fingers felt a stickiness that wasn't sea water, and he flinched with the pain of it.

'Oh, my God,' she whimpered, fingers trembling as they explored the jagged edges of the wounds on his calf.

'It isn't as bad as it looks,' he grunted. 'I think she wasn't all that sure of what she was doing.' He tried to lever himself upright, but Verna leapt to her own feet and pushed him back down again.

'You don't move,' she cried. 'I must clean that, bandage it.'

'With what? I'm not going to die on you, my love,' he said with growing steadiness. 'Now just help me up and we'll go into the water together and wash off the blood, all right?'

'Don't you dare move,' she replied. 'I'll bandage it with my T-shirt.' And in one motion she had stripped off the garment and tensed herself to rip it into strips.

Con's eyes dropped from her face to where her bared breasts gleamed white against the darkness of her tan, and Verna felt a flicker of embarrassment. But it didn't matter; she tensed herself again to rip up the T-shirt.

'No!' His voice halted her and she stood in shock as he spun to his feet and took the T-shirt from her hands before she could tear it.

'Not this one,' he said with a curious gentleness. 'Not ever this one. Please put it back on.' He held the garment as Verna struggled back into it, and while she wanted to argue with him, she didn't.

'Why not this one?' she exclaimed, and then her eyes followed his own down to her heaving bosom, and she knew. Even upside down and inside out, she could easily read the logo.   HELP CURE VIRGINITY

And when she looked up to meet his eyes, her own mirrored the laughter she saw there. She'd bought that T-shirt years before, and had never summoned up the nerve to wear it or the right moment to throw it away.

'That one is mine,' he said. 'I don't care if I bleed to death without it.'

His arms reached out to close her within them, and as their lips sealed her acceptance of his wishes, Verna found herself bubbling with a contented laughter of her own.

They walked into the sea together, and although Verna knew Con really didn't need the help, she was glad that he could lean on her as if he did. His powerful hands ripped the back pocket from his cut-offs and she used that, not her T-shirt, to sponge away the blood and reveal that he'd been right after all; the injuries weren't all that serious, although he winced with pain and made a terrible show of being mortally wounded.

They made the slow trip up the beach in silence, content simply with the touch of each other, and it wasn't until they'd reached the house and slipped quietly in through the back door that he whispered a warning not to waken Madeline.

'All she'll do is start abusing me again, even with you here,' he said. 'And while I admit that I deserve every bit of it and more, I'd rather take it from you. I love you, Verna, and I know that's no excuse, but I ...'

'You'll shut up and let me tend your wounds, that's what you'll do,' she hissed. 'And no arguments, either.'

Con started to object, but subsided immediately when Verna hissed to Sheba, who was observing the bandaging with great interest.

'I'm going to regret ever training her for you,' he said. 'I already do, if you want the truth.'

'If you don't shut up and lie still, you'll regret it even more that you invented Dragon Lady the Editor,' Verna hissed with mock seriousness. 'Because she lives, you know, and she's going to be part of your life for ever.'

'Owww!' he cried as she pressed too hard on the deepest puncture. 'You were a better nurse before.'

'Well, as soon as it's some kind of civilised time, you're

going in for a tetanus shot,' she replied. 'And I'm coming along just to watch them stick the needle in.'

'You're vindictive!'

'True, but I love you. And I don't want you to be limping at the wedding.'

Con sat up abruptly, his large hands reaching out to take Verna by the shoulders. 'Now see here, my love,' he growled. 'I still have some say in this. And I have no intention of waiting any longer than I have to to get you properly to the altar. To hell with the leg!'

'I was thinking of Madeline's wedding,' she replied with a grin, leaning forward to plant a quick kiss on his forehead.

'Well, don't! Because ours will come long before the eighteenth of March,' he said.

'You have to give a month's notice of intent if you're going to use a marriage celebrant,' Verna replied haughtily. 'I checked. And that means that if you start everything off bright and early tomorrow—today—we'll be just in time to make it a double wedding.'

'Your wish is my command,' he nodded, 'but do we really have to wait that long? Surely I can arrange a special licence or something. There has to be a way.'

'From now on, any manipulating you want to do with *my* life, you'll have to get *my* permission first,' Verna replied stoutly. 'Besides, I rather fancy a double wedding, and Madeline would too.'

She leaned down to kiss him yet again, her mouth lingering this time on the bridge of his nose before sliding lower to meet his lips, and when they broke apart, Con shook his head in exaggerated indignation.

'I'll rue the day you ever met Madeline,' he said. 'She'll tell you all my secrets and teach you all *her* bad habits.'

'I already know all your secrets ... except one,' Verna

replied. 'And I'll know that one, too, before I go anywhere near an altar with you, Con Bradley.'

She shivered as Con ran his fingers over her shoulders and then traced intricate designs along the small of her back as his lips moved like velvet around her neck and nipped at her ears.

'Dragon Lady, hmmm. I'll bet I could turn you into a little sugar dragon if I tried,' he whispered. 'And I will too, as soon as my war wounds are healed.'

'And as soon as we're married,' Verna breathed in his ear, her body shivering with the delights of his touch as he turned her so his fingers could trace along the letters of her T-shirt. It was some time before she could speak again.

'Con ...'

'What?' His voice was muffled by the pressure of his lips against her neck.

'I want you to tell me honestly ... was it you on the beach that first morning?'

'What do you think?' he whispered softly in her ear.

'I think I want you to admit it,' she whispered in reply.

'Will you marry me if I don't?' His hands were still following the letters, and Verna could feel herself melting into him.

'No ... well, maybe ... yes. Oh yes,' she cried as her defences crumbled.

Con's whoop of triumph sounded like a drum in her ear, and he thrust her away from him, holding her like a child in his great hands. His eyes glittered with a soft gentle passion that softened even more as his love poured into them.

'All you have to do is ask Sheba,' he said with a wry grin.

Verna looked across the room to where the dog lay, huge red tongue lolling in her silent laughter.

'I don't care anyway,' she said with a saucy grin of her own. 'Every girl should be allowed her fantasies. I'll keep that one for when you're horrid to me.'

'Well, personally I wouldn't believe anything that dog told me anyway,' Con laughed, hauling Verna back into his lap and crushing her with his arms. 'She's the most untrustworthy little mongrel I've ever seen!'

Harlequin Plus

ALL ABOUT DRAGONS

When Con Bradley referred to Verna as a "snaggle-toothed, sulphur-breathing" dragon, small wonder she was horrified. Just for fun, we thought we'd let readers know a bit more about these mythical monsters....

The dragon is a large reptilian creature, sometimes breathing fire, sometimes having wings. It is the oldest member of a mythical monster family that also includes unicorns and griffins. Since recorded history began, it has been sung about, written about, sculpted and painted.

How big is a dragon? Full-grown, it is said to be 150 feet long or as large as a person's fears—whichever is greater! How to recognize one? Look for a blood-red or metallic green complexion; two legs or four, each having long and sharp claws; a shiny, scale-covered body that ends in a long and deadly tail; eyes that are great and bulging; and a long snout. Check, too, for a forked tongue and watch out for the dangerous spike on its nose!

Where do dragons live? Anywhere in the world, and generally in swamps and mountain caves; after all, they're storm demons and rulers of the underground.

But for the most part, the dragon is best known for guarding treasures and devouring fair maidens. And the dragon loses battles with heroes and saints like Beowulf and St. George.

Now we don't think Con ever thought Verna was as bad as all this... but he certainly enjoyed himself making her wonder!

Harlequin Presents...

Romance novels that speak
the language of love known to
women the world over.

Harlequin Presents...

A distinctive series of dramatic
love stories created
especially for you
by world-acclaimed
authors.

DISCOVER...

SUPERROMANCE

From the publisher that understands
how you feel about love.

Almost 400 pages of outstanding
romance reading in every book!

SUPERROMANCE

Longer, exciting, sensual and dramatic!

Here is a golden opportunity to order any or all of the first four great SUPERROMANCES

SUPERROMANCE #1
END OF INNOCENCE
Abra Taylor

They called him El Sol, golden-haired star of the bullring. Liona was proud and happy to be his fiancée...until a tragic accident threw her to the mercies of El Sol's forbidding brother, a man who despised Liona almost as much as he wanted her....

SUPERROMANCE #2
LOVE'S EMERALD FLAME
Willa Lambert

The steaming jungle of Peru was the stage for their love. Diana Green, a spirited and beautiful young journalist, who became a willing pawn in a dangerous game...and Sloane Hendriks, a lonely desperate man driven by a secret he would reveal to no one.

SUPERROMANCE #3
THE MUSIC OF PASSION
Lynda Ward

The handsome Kurt von Kleist's startling physical resemblance to her late husband both attracted and repelled Megan—because her cruel and selfish husband had left in her a legacy of fear and distrust of men. How was she now to bear staying in Kurt's Austrian home? Wouldn't Kurt inflict even more damage on Megan's heart?

SUPERROMANCE #4
LOVE BEYOND DESIRE
Rachel Palmer

Robin Hamilton, a lovely New Yorker working in Mexico, suddenly found herself enmeshed in a bitter quarrel between two brothers—one a headstrong novelist and the other a brooding archaeologist. The tension reached breaking point when Robin recognized her passionate, impossible love for one of them....

COMPLETE AND MAIL THE COUPON ON THE FOLLOWING PAGE TODAY!